Cover Art by Dom
Inquiries:
443-574-5889
dominiclapi@hotmail.com

THE BOOK

n the year 2016, a young woman in Florida receives
erious packages on her doorstep. In 2076, a man is
and left out in the unforgiving Antarctic elements.
016, a private investigator is on the case. In 2076,
United Nation's top international detective is on the
. Only together will they realize how the two myster-
re connected, and what that means for the future of
nanity!

THE LAST KNIFE

THE LAST KNIFE

DOMINIC LAPI

CONTENTS

CHAPTER I

THE YEAR 2016

Her legs went up to the ceiling, and so did her problems.

It was midday. I had come in dripping from the lazy pattering of a springtime rainfall. When I was halfway to my worn armchair, she entered the room.

"May I help you?" I asked the blonde, more than a little perturbed.

"From what I hear, you're the only one who can," she said, closing the office door and taking a few brisk steps, stopping in front of my cluttered desk.

She had a cool demeanor, but the unfocused look in her eye complemented the faint wavering of her voice. I glanced at her for a moment. She was mostly bouncy blonde curls and an excellent sense of fashion. Her outfit was punctuated by bold high heels.

"Well then, have a seat," I said, taking my own, and now much more accepting of the intrusion. "Where were you? It looks like you've been waiting a while, but I did not see you when I came in."

"How'd you know I've been waiting?"

"It's been raining for an hour at least, yet you have not a drop on you, and um..." I leaned slowly over, to the side of the desk, peering with my dark brows raised, "...no umbrella."

She pursed her red lips. "Well, a gentleman could've lent me his umbrella, you know, walking here."

A slow grin crept across my face without permission. She was testing me. I did have a bit of a reputation after all. It was only fair. "The ends of your hair are still a little damp. And, seeing as how it had been raining all this morning, I doubt you left the house in a sleeveless blouse." I leaned back in my chair, putting my feet up on the little cubbyhole at the bottom of my desk. "And the yellow raincoat in the lobby seems to match your shoes and purse pretty well."

"Maybe I was in the bathroom."

"There is no bathroom on this floor. You wouldn't have time to make it back without my seeing you."

She uncrossed her arms and un-scrunched her tiny nose. "Okay, okay. Your assistant let me wait in his office because it had a fan. I'm not really used to this Florida heat yet."

I combed my brown hair back, still slick with cloud tears. "Sorry about that. I have been meaning to put a fan out there in the lobby. And his office is..."

She smiled. "A supply closet?"

"Yeah," I said with a chuckle.

The woman opened her mouth to speak but was interrupted by a succession of rapid knocks at the door, followed by an excited "Nate?!"

"Come on in, Sam," I said with a sigh.

Sam, a soaking wet, rotund man with shaggy hair, burst through the door, creating a puddle in my doorway that I was sure to slip on at some point. "Nate, I..." He trailed off as his eyes met those of the lovely young woman whose name I had yet to glean. He gestured toward her, "Oh, I'm sorry boss, it's just that she was waiting for you, and, and—"

"It's alright Sam. Next time just wait for me to come back."

"I went to get you next door, but you'd already left."

I followed his gaze and saw the cell phone I left behind to charge near the window. Sam wiped his brow, slick with the rain, sweat, or both, and with a quick nod to the both of us, closed the door.

"So," I said as the woman turned back toward me, "Miss..."

"Oh, sorry! Liza Berkley." She rose to shake my hand.

"You can call me Nate," I said. "Why do you need a PI?"

After our obligatory handshake, she picked her handbag off the floor and put it in her lap, placing a hand over it before she spoke. "Last week I... Well um, okay, my grandmother died last month. I was the last relative she had, and she left me her house and her belongings."

"Money?" I asked.

"The little bit she had left, yeah, she left to me.

I moved into the house on the sixteenth. I had a graphic design job in New York, but I'm thinking about staying here for a while." She shrugged, "I've been wanting to freelance. But every week," she began, fumbling around, trying to pull something from her handbag, "I have been getting packages on the front stoop. Once or twice a week since I got here."

Liza removed a glittering golden elephant from its home in her bag and handed it to me gingerly. It was heavy. Sensing there was more to the story, I put it down on the desk, took a cloth from my drawer, and picked it up again, turning it over with two hands, careful not to touch it directly. "Looks expensive," I said, making a note of its dimensions. *About the size of a piggybank.*

"Yeah it is. They all are. I had it appraised. It's made of lead with twenty-four-karat gold casing, inlaid with amethyst. Like the others, there was no return address and I want to know where these are coming from."

"Maybe you just have a secret admirer," I said, shaking the thing gently, then a little less so. "Are they addressed to you? Do you still have the packages- err, packaging?"

Liza started chewing on her nail a bit. "I didn't really think to keep them. I just have the one for this," she said, gesturing toward the golden beast, "and it's a bit ripped up."

Miraculously, she pulled yet another oddity from her infinitely spacious handbag; this time, a flattened cardboard box emerged. I threw some stuff on the floor to make more room for the elephant and the sad, water-damaged square that was once a proud box. It had stopped raining for the moment and golden sunlight filtered through the window, bouncing off Liza's yellow hair and the glittering elephant in similar fashion. The delivery address was printed onto a card and taped to the box's creased brown cardboard. The address read:

Liza Berkley
3719 Crestmont Ave
Tampa, Florida 33619

The return address was the same as the delivery address.

"Well, this person certainly knows who you are," I said, admittedly losing some interest in such an apparently harmless case.

"Actually, the first ones were just addressed to 'Resident.' Only the last three had my name."

"Hm, that implies that the sender may not have known who you were when you first moved in. Do you know at all if your grandmother received packages like these?"

She wrinkled her narrow nose. "I really have no idea. I hadn't seen her in about a year. I mean, not that I really know of. But she did have some new trinkets and centerpieces that I hadn't seen before."

I fumbled a little in my drawer and took out my trusty notepad. As I jotted down some of the more pertinent details I asked, "And how many have you gotten so far?"

"This is number six."

"Six! All elephants?"

"No, they're all sorts of things. Here." Suddenly remembering, she quickly took out her phone and began queuing photos. I reached for it politely and began a thorough inspection.

"I would have brought them, but I wanted to see if you would take my case, or if it was even worth investigating."

On her phone, I had already scrolled past an ornately designed miniature lamp and a simple clock, when she continued her story.

"The reason I'm so concerned with this is, ever since I've moved in, I feel like," she paused, moving awkwardly in her chair, "I'm being watched, or followed, or something. I can hear noises outside the house and the other day, I saw footprints in the yard.

"And last night," at this her breath caught for a moment, "I saw a man's face in the kitchen window. He was gone so quickly; I wasn't sure I saw him in the first place. But after everything that happened, I was terrified, alone in that big house, so I called the police."

I put down the phone next to the box. "You did the right thing. What did they say?"

"They said it didn't look like anyone had been there and they didn't see anyone. They suggested I invest in more home security, keep the doors locked, take a picture, and call again if I need to."

I sat quietly for a few minutes looking at the images on Liza's phone. These included a bouquet of glass flowers in a metal vase, a puppet, and an—alive baby chimpanzee in a miniature bathtub? Realizing I had scrolled too far, I went back to the beginning and found a kitchen radio. "Okay, Ms. Berkley," I said, standing, "I charge $50 an hour, and I do not work Saturdays. Are you okay with that?"

She nodded and smiled. "Fine with me. I just want this to be done with."

I walked over to the window, and as I began to look out, it started raining again. So, I went back to the comfort of my armchair, designed specifically for rainy days. "Look, I don't mean to sound insensitive, but this is a pretty standard stalker-case. I should have it wrapped up in no time. The fact that this guy is sticking around makes my job much easier."

Liza leaned back in her chair slightly, clearly more at ease.

"Let's start at the beginning." My notepad was ready. "I need names. Ex-lovers, un-tipped pizza guys, family. Was anyone else expecting the inheritance?"

"No, I am the only family she had left."

"Nothing? No third cousins or extra friendly nurses who worked with your grandma?"

"No, she was in near perfect health as far as I know. It was just me, my mom and my grandma living together after Grandpa passed. But my mom and Grandma had a falling-out and we moved away. My mom died two years ago this month."

"Hm. Any relationships you had that went sour? Ugly breakups?"

"Nothing," she said, betraying no emotion.

I gave her a look. "Nothing?"

"No, not really. The last guy I saw was named Josh. That was a year ago."

"Josh what?"

"Ushman, U-S-H-M-A-N. Josh Ushman. He moved away for work and we decided not to see each other anymore."

"Who decided?" I asked, writing his name down next to a note that read: *sparkly piggy bank.*

"He did, mostly. He got a job in San Francisco."

I closed my notepad and put my feet in the desk's cubbyhole once more. "Well, look. There are a few ways to go about this. I could take this murdered cardboard box, and the next parcel that inevitably comes your way, and try to have them traced back to the source through the Postal Service, but since no crime has been committed, I doubt that would be a fruitful endeavor. And if this person were smart, he could have used a remailer service that would use the postmark of any of the service's facilities. It would be untraceable and anonymous. There is a place right here in Old Town that I've dealt with before. They completely shred any documents that aren't going to be mailed. I think instead, we shoul—"

Liza put her hand to her forehead as a prelude to her interruption of my brilliant lecture. "Oh, right, so that's the other thing that worried me, I forgot to tell you. Yesterday I spoke to my mail-woman about the packages. She said that she's been on her route since before I even moved here, and she never delivered any packages."

Surprised, I took another look at the cardboard. "Well, it does not seem... It looks like it went through USPS, not a shipping company or a vendor..." With a start, I banged my fist on the table, startling Liza. "Well there we go! We solved the case."

With a smug expression, I reached for my coffee mug to finish it off, but, was dissatisfied when a cold, bitter swig greeted my palate and my palate's palate.

"How?" Liza asked fervently.

"This person is going through the trouble of

making these packages look officially delivered so that you are more likely to open them. All we have to do is put a camera near the door, and we'll see him delivering them himself. Or, if this person is especially crafty, he'll hire someone to do it. Either way, we will eventually find our man. Is there any regularity to the delivery of these packages?"

"I don't think so. They've all come at different times and days during the week."

"Hm, that will make it more difficult to confront him if the camera cannot catch his face. But you thought they were coming in the mail, so, would you say these packages are usually arriving midday?"

She shrugged. "I honestly have no idea. But I always brought them in when I got the mail. Either coming home or going out."

"Well, for now, let's assume early mail hours and work from there. We can set up cameras at the door and the windows and rig them with motion detectors to alert us when our guy comes. I can lend you my personal equipment if you want. Or you could buy a system yourself. Either me or Sam will be waiting nearby during that time to follow anyone who leaves a box. Is there anyone in the neighborhood you trust? Any sweet old ladies across the street that can help keep an eye out?"

She gave a little sigh. "Just one, but she's way at the end of the street. I don't know the other neighbors very well. Or at all really."

"That's fine. For all we know it is one of your neighbors. Or the mailwoman for that matter."

"I thought you thought it was a guy?"

"That's if your man in the window is connected to the packages. He might not be. He might be a lover of your grandmother who was not informed of her passing. Or maybe it was just an ugly woman. But that is why you hired me to find out for sure. Now, is there a time I can come by this week to set everything up and take a look at those other gifts you received?"

"You can come tomorrow. I have a meeting with an advertising firm from 11:00 to 2:45, so you can come by around 3 p.m."

"Alright, sounds good. Give me one sec." I put my trusty notepad back in its place and shouted, "SAM!" After a moment, shuffling could be heard outside the door. Sam came in so quickly he almost tripped. "Yeah, uh, yes?"

"3:00 tomorrow?"

"I don't think you have anything, Nate. Let me double check." He looked through the calendar on his phone. "Nope. I guess that means you have something now?"

I gave my new client a wink. "I sure do."

————————————

The next day, I was waiting outside next to the Nate-mobile, sweating through my purple T-shirt, and watching an enormous white crane waddle down the sidewalk. "Sam, you ready yet?" I yelled. The crane looked up at me as if I were disturbing it, then went back about its business.

"Coming!" Sam hurried out the door, his hair moist with perspiration. He locked it, struggling with the camera equipment under his arm. He threw it in the back of my truck, and we were off. He said, "Ms. Berkley called. She said she was running a couple minutes late and she'd meet us there. She'll probably get there the same time we will." He wiped his brow with a handkerchief or something, then stuffed it back in his cargo shorts.

"Okay," I said. "I looked into this Josh Ushman character. His social media accounts place him in San Francisco, so we can cross him off for now."

We pulled up to the address just before 3 p.m. It

was a beautifully designed four-bedroom, Mediter-
ranean style house with a red tile roof and a small
porch. The bright blue trim around the doors and
windows gave it a unique appearance compared to
that of its neighbors. It sat in a neighborhood of
only six houses, each generously spaced and surrounded by a thick grove of trees. Behind the trees
was a fenced off body of water. Two of the six
houses were directly across the road from Liza's.

"This one is for sale," I said pointing to the one
on the left and opening the truck door.

"Look, I think that's her," Sam said, pointing
to the expensive red car pulling up behind us.

Liza's fair skin glowed blindingly in the sunlight as she walked over to meet us. Her taste in
clothing was impeccable as before. "Hey guys. The
other things I got in the mail are right inside. I left
them alone like you said."

"Okay," I replied, taking a long look around
to see if anyone was watching. It seemed quiet. "I
want to take a look around the yard if that is alright. Sam, you can start with the cameras."

He nodded and I began my inspection of the
bushes in the front yard, making my way slowly to
the kitchen window on the left side of the house.

Suddenly, I heard Liza shriek, "OH MY GOD!" and Sam call my name. I ran back to the front door and saw them standing just inside. I pushed past Sam and tried to piece together what had happened. The place was trashed. The coat rack next to the door had been tipped over and some of the jackets were inside out, as if they had been rifled through. The bookshelf on the right side of the door was turned over, but the books were scattered, not piled together. They looked like they had been thrown on the floor one by one. Next to the bookshelf, the spacious living room had its couch cushions torn, its television gutted, its rug balled into a huddled mass, its pictures taken down, and its shelves left barren. To the left of the entrance, the open kitchen was a no man's land, its floor covered in spilled cereal boxes, refrigerator racks, broken jars, empty trash bags, and pots and pans. All the cabinets were open, and the doors next to the stairs, directly across from the entrance, were open as well. The backdoor behind the stairs was ajar, not able to shut with a flowerpot in its way.

"Vandalism," Sam whispered.

"No, Sam. Somebody was looking for something. Liza, call the police and do not move or touch anything yet. I need to look around. Sam, those tracks should lead out to the tree line. Run around back and see if we can catch anyone still leaving. If not, come back and start taking pictures before the cops show up."

I took a few steps, following and avoiding the muddy tracks and footprints left on the tile. The perpetrator had come in through the back door, doubled back, gone up the stairs, and then left the way he came.

As Liza fished her phone out of her bag, I took out my tape measure to make a measurement of the clearest boot print. But I froze, because at that moment, I looked up, and behind a balled-up blanket, I saw it.

"Wait! Don't call yet."

"What, why?" Liza's finger was poised over her phone, still ready to attack. Her eyes were watery. Clearly, she was not having a good day.

"Over there," I pointed to an ornately designed miniature lamp which was still plugged in and untouched. "Is that the lamp that came in the mail?"

"Um yes. Why?" Her face was beet red and her voice shook.

"Liza, I need you to think. Did anyone, anyone at all know what time you would be gone today? Did you tell anyone?"

She slowly lowered the phone. "No. Just you and your assistant."

"And the people with whom you were meeting?"

"They told me I could come in any time before five. I had a few errands to run after that. So, kinda. Not really."

"Okay, stay there, but tell me where you put each thing that came in the mail."

"There's the lamp, uh, you have the elephant, the flowers are in the main bedroom on the dresser, the clock is in the hall, and the radio is in the bathroom, no wait, it's in the kitchen."

"And the puppet?"

"Oh, I think I threw that in the closet. The upstairs closet in the hall."

"I will be right back." I passed a living room clock which was on the floor, its back removed. In the hallway however, the clock I recognized from its photo was still on the wall. Upstairs, the main bedroom's drawers were all removed, with clothes strewn every which way. The glass flowers in their metal pot and a TV remote were the only things left on the dresser, which according to marks on the carpet, had clearly been moved and put back into place. As I saw each familiar object, unmoved and unmolested, a knot grew in my stomach. The upstairs closet was open, and the only thing that remained on its high shelf was a wooden puppet who stared down at me unblinkingly. I went downstairs as I heard Sam coming back in and looked over my right shoulder to see the radio perched on the counter, its antenna high.

"Find anything?" Sam asked, taking pictures of the floor.

I looked into Liza's terrified eyes and kicked myself for not realizing sooner what might have been going on. "It was the elephant, Sam. The elephant she gave us. It was the only way he could have known when she would be gone and how much time he had to search. Go ahead and call the police Liza, they will probably welcome my help on this one."

CHAPTER II

THE YEAR 2076

"How much longer?" asked Nigel, picking his nose.

The automatic pilot responded in monotone fashion. "The jet needs to refuel its solar cells in the upper atmosphere. That will take at least one hour. Once complete, we will descend and arrive within twenty minutes." The computer's voice sounded from every corner of the cabin, then went silent.

"Greeaat..." Nigel stood up and walked across the cabin, stooping to look through the tiny viewports as he passed them, admiring the dense clouds that looked as if they could support his weight.

He came to the back of the plane and spent an inordinate amount of time at the bathroom mirror pulling up his shirt to admire his abdominal muscles from different angles. *Lookin' good,* he thought. He pushed back his thick black hair and winked at himself, exiting the restroom. He looked around at all the empty seats and slumped down into the only one in which he had never sat. It was comfy.

Without warning, the plane jolted forward, almost jostling Nigel out of his seat. "What the hell was that?"

"We are beginning decent. Please fasten safety belts."

"Okay people, you heard him!" Nigel said to an empty cabin.

A half an hour later, the plane set gently down on a wide and barren sheet of ice.

Nigel leaned, looking out of his viewport, studying the hazy wasteland of snowy foreboding. In the distance, he could see some vague shapes, darker than the snow, and a few lights built to penetrate its vast obscurity.

"You couldn't have parked a little closer?"

This time, there was no response from the onboard computer navigation system.

"Awesome." Nigel took a thick blue coat with

fur trim, matching gloves, and a sturdy pair of boots from the overhead compartment and awkwardly put them on.

Taking a deep breath, he told the door to open and descended into the blinding white abyss.

Two people stood outside the plane, a man and a woman, sporting much bulkier clothing. Assaulted by the cold, Nigel turned on the heater in his coat to its automatic setting, so it would measure and regulate his body's temperature in order to keep it consistent.

"Greetings!" shouted the woman with a thick Russian accent. The wind was picking up, making it harder to see and hear. "Come this way," she said. "My name is Catherine, this is Oslow. He does not speak English so well. With wind, it is too loud here for the translators, but inside will be better."

"Hi friend," said Oslow, an amiable-looking man with round, soft features.

They trudged ahead, stopping at a hydroelectric snowmobile fifty feet from the jet. As they mounted the vehicle, Nigel said, "My name is detective Nigel Woods." He was not sure if they had heard him, since they began driving as he started to speak.

In no time, they arrived at the Antarctic research base. A Russian flag was painted over a tall, circular building with enormous floodlights attached on all sides. A massive tower composed of antennas of all different sizes and shapes, and a radar dish, jutted from the center of the building. Attached to the main building were two smaller buildings of similar construction. All three were built on a complex system of elevated stilts, giving the buildings the ridiculous appearance of being able to walk off at any moment. Which, in a way, they could.

Clustered on one side of the base, cheap ready-made housing units littered the surrounding landscape. They were identical squat cubes, maybe two hundred or so, aligned in perfect rows, lit by poles, fires, and smaller lights attached to each structure. As Nigel squinted at them, he realized more were being erected.

"Welcome to Russia Base 14," said the woman as their vehicle slowed to a stop. Despite the wind and snow, Nigel could make out scores of people moving in between the housing units.

They led him inside the main building which was covered from top to bottom with outdated computers and equipment. It was a round, open space, with a humongous central heating unit attached to the ceiling. It had ventilation hoses wide enough to fit two people, that snaked downward from the ceiling along the walls and into the floor. Near the back of the room, two men played cards, near the front, everyone was hard at work looking at one screen or another. In all, twenty men and women stopped what they were doing and looked up as Nigel entered the room. Nigel kept his coat on but turned off his heater.

"It will be warmer soon," said Oslow, talking through an instantaneous microphone translator on his collar.

"Yes," nodded Catherine. "Our coldest season is near ended."

"Wonderful," Nigel replied. He was still taking stock of the room, which made him feel uncomfortable and depressed, though it was better than most of the places he had been sent. And it maybe had a sort of coziness to it. Still, there were much nicer Antarctic colonies. "Now where's the—"

A scrawny man approached, forcefully frowning. "Who's this then?" he asked, addressing Catherine in a painfully British accent.

"Carl, this is the detective."

"It's about bloody time. Only one of you?"

"Just me," said Nigel, holding up his badge with the United Nation's officer seal.

This only served to deepen Carl's frown. "UN detective? I thought they were sending a Russian."

Nigel sighed, not wanting to spend any more time than he had to in the land of misfit toys. "Antarctica is UN jurisdiction. Everywhere but Antarctikorea."

"But I thought Russia didn't allow UN polic—"

"Well you thought wrong. Russia has to play ball just like everyone else down here."

Carl adjusted his pee-green turtleneck and crossed his arms. "Whatever, as long as you do your job."

Nigel could tell Carl was a little rattled by what had happened but decided not to care. "I would, but I'm still standing here, aren't I?"

"Oh-kay," Catherine breathed, stepping between the two who were both glowering. "We can show you, to get you started." She held her arm out, leading Nigel further into the building. Right this way."

The three of them, Nigel, Catherine, and Oslow, walked through the center of the room, past the men playing cards (who looked a little disappointed upon seeing Nigel) and through a tight corridor which led to another circular room, smaller than the last.

This room, unlike the central chamber, appeared to be a utility room that also housed maintenance equipment. Its ceiling was high and rose even higher at its center. The ventilation tubes and pipes from the other room were apparently attached to the new room as well, coming through the center of the ceiling and making their way back to the ground. Some branched off and led back out the corridor.

The group walked straight through to the other side of the room and stopped just before the backdoor. On the floor beside the door was a yellow tarp and a puddle of water.

"We kept everyone out," said Catherine.

Nigel looked Catherine up and down. She had short brown hair, wrinkles enough to show her wisdom, and she looked tired. But not just tired from lack of sleep, it was a tired in her bones. She was five foot two and must not have weighed more than a hundred pounds. "And what is it you do here?" Nigel asked her.

"I'm ranking supervisor."

"Of the entire colony?"

"No, this was first a scientific research base. I started work here when we were just the ten of us. After the climate changing, we opened the base up for the migrants, but Russian government kept funding our research team. This is still functioning base, and I am in charge of everything goes on."

"And what is it you research?" This was a question to which Nigel already knew the answer from his briefing.

"We measure effects that the globally increasing temperature has on Antarctic, and secondarily, we try to develop more, er, how do you say, economic? Economic solutions than what is already offered."

"Your English is pretty good, makes my job easier. And Oslow?" Nigel gestured to get his attention. "What do you do?"

After a pause during which Oslow's translator repeated the question back in Russian, he said, "I am a glaciologist. I measure calving ice shelves. But I now also oversee the new people coming to live here and help them adjust. Not all are Russian, but we make sure they have a place to stay. It's danger-ous here alone."

Nigel sniffed. "Right, well, now that I know who I'm talking to, we can get down to business. I'll need a list of residents from you, and Catherine, your staff register. Oslow, you can start getting that ready for me, and Catherine, I'll talk to you alone."

As Oslow walked off, Nigel took a small, egg-shaped device from out of his pocket and started to fiddle with it. He looked up at Catherine for a few seconds, then back down at the device. "Well?" he asked. "Come on then. Tell me what happened. We're losing daylight."

"Oh, I am sorry detective. Oslow, while alone, found Anton outside this door, prostrate in the snow. He brought Anton in here, and brought the doctor who examined him, found him dead."

Nigel lifted the shiny round device he had been adjusting, and it began to hover in the air. After a moment, it moved off slowly, scanning its sur-roundings in order to form one complete 3D panoramic picture. "No, don't do that," Nigel ex-claimed, with an air of exasperation as Catherine bent to lift the tarp. "Just, just stand over there. Better yet, go get the doctor for me."

She walked away, stepping gingerly. Nigel put on his gloves and cracked open the huge metal door behind the tarp with its vaguely human-sized lump. The wind was loud, and the snowfall had picked up considerably. He shut the door, sliding it horizontally, deciding to tackle the outside from outside, going around the building once he was finished indoors.

The hovering device returned to Nigel's open palm, and he reset it to scan for DNA and fingerprints by identifying, then separating sets of chemical compounds. It floated off. Then, he squatted down, carefully removing the tarp to inspect the body of Anton which lay underneath. He took a small manual DNA sample, to send off to United Nation headquarters for ID confirmation.

A portly, reddish faced man came in, approaching the crime scene, followed closely by Catherine.

"Ah, ah, ah," said Nigel without turning. "No more stepping. That's far enough. You're the doc?" He was still crouched in front of the body, his back to them.

Catherine spoke, "This is Dr. Jakobi. He's been many years here, a trusted colleague."

"Hello sir. You wanted to see me?" spoke the doctor.

"Of course, I did. You're the doc, doc. You sure he's dead?"

Doctor Jakobi glanced down at the blueish, popsicle of a man whose head was twisted completely around to look up at them, while the front of his body was face-down, flat on the floor. The doctor grumbled darkly, "Yes," clearly not amused.

"Well, we're on the same page there, pal. What's your diagnosis?"

"It was a cervical fracture of the C2 that caused a spinal cord injury: instant death. He also had a large scalp contusion, but it didn't seem to damage the skull. The contusion made me think there was a struggle."

"Yeah, well, that's for me to decide," Nigel replied. He diverted his attention away from the body for a moment to examine the puddle of water about six feet long, leading to the door. "Do you people often track in so much snow?"

Catherine replied, "Not so much as that, usually, but this was special circumstance. But yes, we often bring in outside snow during the winter times."

"By the time Oslow dragged him in, he was already covered," added the doctor.

"If it was snowing outside, why wasn't he wearing a coat?"

There was no response.

"Was there a blizzard? A lot of wind or anything?"

"No, the weather did not turn until today," answered Catherine.

Nigel looked down at Anton. He was an enormous man, built like a workhorse. Anyone who killed him would need tremendous strength to break his thickly muscular neck, but the stealth of a ninja, it being almost impossible to sneak up on someone in snow. Nigel tried to search the man's clothing, cracking the somehow still frozen fabric in some places. He noticed two large carabiners attached to his belt. The pair behind him waited patiently. Then he asked, "And does anyone know why this dude's pockets are all empty?"

The doctor replied, "Are they? Perhaps whoever stole his belongings killed him."

Nigel stood. "Hey! Sherlock! I don't need your input. Let me do my job, and don't let any of these schlubs overhear you either." The robotic device that Nigel had released upon its short journey, finished its task and returned to Nigel, who viewed the projection it displayed on its top. He then put it away. "I'm gonna need prints from everyone who has access to this room. I'm assuming you need some sort of biometric ID to get in?"

"No, just identification key," Catherine replied.

As she spoke, Nigel took out another device to scan the body. He slowly waved it around, stopping at the neck, where he held it longer, looking at a tiny screen. He then put it away. "Which I assume he doesn't have anymore. Can you track the keys at all?"

Catherine shook her head. "No, not that I think."

"Of course not," Nigel muttered to himself. "Anyway, I need those prints. Even if you have them on record, or whatever. Do 'em again. Doc, I'm putting you in charge, since you're so eager to help with the investigation. Here." He handed the doctor a long cylindrical device for the task.

The doctor hesitated for more than a moment, glaring intensely. Then he took the device and walked off without speaking.

"Any cameras in here?" Nigel asked.

Once again, Catherine was the bearer of un-helpful news. "No, not in this part. Only... no, no cameras."

"Um okay. What was that bit before the pause?"

"I'm sorry?"

"You were gonna say something."

"No, I had nothing else."

A pause. "Whatever. And what did Anton do? Y'know his job? He worked in here, right?"

"He worked in every building. He came earlier this year. He is engineer. He worked on heating and other system maintaining."

"Uh huh." Nigel was slowly walking around the room now, stopping and starting every so of-ten. Finally, he stopped in front of Catherine. "Did you know him well?"

"Oh yes, Anton was joy. He always had a каламбур to tell. A, joke that plays with words."

"Did he have anybody he was sweet on? Any hook-ups or family here with him?"

"No one, no. He had a wife, but she is travel-ling."

"Enemies? Rival coworkers?"

"Not that I think of."

"Hm. Lot of good that does me." Nigel pointed toward the door. "I want to go around. I don't wanna step on any boot prints."

"Okay, this way, with me."

Catherine directed two security personnel to stand guard over the room. Then, they walked back through the corridor and into the central chamber. Everyone seemed to have resumed his or her work, and Nigel walked with expedience, to avoid gaining the workers' attention once again. They went through a hallway and through a door that let out on the right side of the round structure whence they came in. As Nigel was zipping up his coat, preparing to step through the door and out into the unforgiving white, Oslow approached carry a tablet computer. "Here you go, detective."

Nigel touched his phone to it which beeped when it finished downloading the resident list. "Thanks," he said. "It's a good thing you're here." Nigel opened the door. "You were the guy who found him, so you're coming with us."

The original trio went back out, mounting another vehicle that took them the short distance to their destination. Thankfully, the wind was not quite as aggressive, dying down enough that they could hear each other.

Above the backdoor (on the other side of which lay Anton) was a small metal overhang that was intended to give an entrant temporary respite from the snow. Unfortunately, it did not seem to be doing much, since the wind was blowing at an alarming angle. It was crowned with snow piled ten feet high, in a way that made Nigel doubt the structure's continued integrity.

Nigel turned his coat's fabric heater back on and trudged forward. "Damn, looks like any boot prints are gone. Where'd you find him, Oz?"

Oslow showed him the spot, just outside the shelter of the overhang. The area around the backdoor was isolated, with nothing to the right of it. The community of shelter houses did not start for such a distance to the left, that they were only visible as gray blurs, specters with glowing eyes being swallowed by the darkening chaotic vastness. "He was here, then I dragged him in through this way. But there was only one set of footprints in the snow."

"Only one? Are you sure?" Nigel could not use his hoverbot to search for bio traces in the storm, so he scanned the doorframe and took prints and samples manually. Photography would have been pointless. In all truth, the overhang helped a little, but it certainly did not stop the snow from coming through and making the process twice as frustrating. When he was finished, Nigel said, "I need this snow dug up so I can see what there is to see. D'ya have anything that can help with that?"

"We can help, I think. Are you remaining here?" asked Catherine.

"Take me back to my plane first. I need some more equipment."

Catherine and Oslow waited outside the plane as Nigel hefted a three-foot radar detector down the plane's steps and onto the snowmobile. It was shaped like a weedwhacker and had a small screen on the top, above the handle. They drove back to the main building where Catherine and Nigel waited for Oslow to return with shovels and heat lamps, then returned to the site of the murder.

Nigel walked around, waving the detector back and forth above the snow to see if anything was hidden beneath.

And indeed, something was.

He pointed to the spot and began to dig. The

snow was hard and frozen underneath the soft upper layer. Thus, Nigel had to wait for the heat lamps to thaw the patch before he could continue. Finally, he broke through and retrieved a collapsible knife, only five or so inches in length from the tip of the very pointy blade to the start of the hilt. It was completely open, and Nigel knew it would not close, being thoroughly frozen. Knowing fingerprints might still be lifted from a wet, nonporous surface, he bagged it.

"Do either of you recognize this?" He tried to hold it in the dim light cast by the bulb over the door.

"A standard knife, utility knife. It can be signed out of quartermaster station," said Catherine. "But Anton was not stabbed, was he?"

Nigel made an almost childishly condescending noise. "He could've been held up with it, had his stuff stolen,"—he made a gruesome gesture—"crk, neck broken, knife dropped." He pointed down at the shallow hole that was already beginning to refill. "Would you say that's a day's worth of snow?"

"Yes, it is likely," said Oslow.

Catherine looked less convinced. "We have

someone to monitor precipitation amount. If you measure, I can tell you."

Nigel measured the depth of the hole. Then, he went over the area again with his weedwhacker. "Oz. Where were his tracks coming from?"

Oslow pointed in an arc toward the group of shelters. "From the town. In the direction of his house quadrant. You can speak with his roommate Alexi."

"His roommate? Wasn't his wife coming back?"

"Unfortunately, because of the equatorial migrations, we have been, um, overpopulated. Too many people, not enough shelters. And she was not coming back for another month."

"Hm. Alexi what?"

"Um..." Oslow grabbed the tablet, clumsily trying to shelter it from the snow. "Here," he said pointing with a fat gloved finger and handing it to Nigel.

"Morozov. Alexi Morozov. Thanks Ozzy. Bump it." Oslow awkwardly bumped Nigel's outstretched fist.

With Oslow's help, Nigel did a lap, painstakingly scanning the entire trajectory of Anton's path with his scanner. After a non-insignificant amount of time, the two of them returned to Catherine who was still by the door. "Nothin,'" Nigel reported. "You said the knife had to be signed out. Does that mean it has a serial number or something?"

"No, not knives. They have nothing. We keep track just of who has them. If they say they lost theirs they must pay or trade for second knife, and we give them new one."

"Well, has anyone reported a missing knife?"

Catherine gave an almost imperceptible shrug under her layers of coat. "You have to ask quartermaster."

"Fine," said Nigel. "Here's what we do now. I need the doc and your security beefcakes to help me with the body. Clear out the building until we're done. While you're doing that, Oz, take me back to my plane one more time."

CHAPTER III

THE YEAR 2016

The police arrived eight minutes later. By then, we were all waiting on the sidewalk so the police could secure the scene. Once they arrived, we were separated so they could take our statements.

"Woah, how ya doin' Nate?" asked Officer Johnson, a man of tremendous proportion. At least a head taller than I, the enormity of his square fingers, linebacker girth, and bushy beard, were all appreciated in equal measure as he shaded me from the harsh afternoon sun. "Haven't seen you 'round the station in a year or so. Been doin' civil cases?"

"It has been quiet. Nothing like 2010."

"Thank god for that. What are you doing here? Ya friends with the lady?"

I could see her down the road talking to another officer. She was keeping it together surprisingly well considering the news I had just given her about what was really going on. "Actually, Liza is a client."

"Oh jeezus, here we go." erupted Johnson. "Go on, ya know the drill. Don't leave anything out."

I caught him up on the events of the past few days. He knew me well enough to let me speak, giving him part oral statement, part exposition, and part setting up my case to convince the department to hire me on, so I could do the job for both them and my client at the same time. After I did, I came to the important bit. "And it was not until just before you got here that I realized she was being recorded. All the stuff she received in the mail, they all had recording devices in them. When you guys are done with prints, I can come in and show you which ones. If we are lucky, they could still be transmitting. And whoever did this is the same person who sent that mail. I have to tell you, I really have no idea where all this is going, but it has me very worried."

Officer Johnson sighed gruffly. "I'll let you do the heavy lifting on this one, Nate. We're spread thin with all the gang stuff. You want to come with me and question the neighbors? I saw a couple of 'em peekin' out already. Then we can bag the cameras and you can give me your written statement."

"It's good to see you again, Phil," I said, extending my hand out toward Officer Johnson.

He gave it a hardy shake and replied, "You too, bud." He punctuated it with a slap on the back that almost knocked me over.

We started walking over to the closest house, the one on the left. Its architectural style was similar to Liza's. I began to ask, "You were planning to document the area canvass for—"

"Four neighbors: left, right, and in front, but we can do 'em all if you want. There's only six."

"Yes, and one is for sale. It looks newly constructed."

He turned to see where I was pointing. "Oh, didn't notice that."

We came to the front door of what, so far, was an immaculately well kempt house. The slotted mailbox by the door was overflowing, but two cars were in the driveway and it looked like people were home. After a knock and announcement, vague noises were heard, and the door was quickly opened.

"Hi officer, what's going on?" said a young man of dark complexion and even darker moustache. He had a thick head of hair, glasses, and a bright pink polo shirt tucked into his khaki cargo shorts. His hairy legs led to bare feet. A woman stalked up behind him. She was a tad shorter than he and had thick chocolatey curls. They both had fresh tan-lines but seemed comfortable in the Floridian climate.

"Hi, I'm Officer Johnson, this is Private Investigator Nathan Gallup. He's helpin' us today. There was a break-in next door. Can we ask you some questions?"

The man put his hand over his moustache. "Oh no, Honey, did you hear that? A break-in just next door."

"Oh Lord, I hope everyone is alright," she replied.

"Of course, we'd be happy to help. Please, come on in." The man had a way of talking that made whatever he said seem disingenuous and overly friendly. But he seemed like a talker, and that was good.

"Anything to drink?" asked the woman.

"Thanks, I am okay," I said walking in. The house had a layout nearly identical to the one I had just left. It was clean and tidy with lots of sunlight pouring in through wide, curtain-less windows. There were a few things scattered here and there, but the people were clearly not participants in the rampant consumerism that so often burdened American households.

"It's just the two of you here?" asked Johnson, grabbing a seat after being led to the kitchen table. The skinny wooden chair he chose made him look even bigger. I sat at the head of the table, and the woman sat next to the man.

"Yes sir, that's correct. For now." The man sat across from Johnson and continued, beaming. "I'm Fernando, this is my wonderful wife Jordan."

I took out my phone and propped it up. "Before we continue, I would like to record you. Is that alright?"

"Oh, yes that's fine," said Fernando.

"Alright," agreed Jordan.

In order to build rapport and develop a sense of their body language and speech patterns when telling the truth, I led with some personal questions. "You have a lovely home. How long have you had it?"

Jordan answered first. She sat stiffly upright, only moving her head to talk to me. "Not long. We've had it a little over a year now. We bought it right after we were married."

"It's a nice area, nice neighborhood?" asked Johnson.

Fernando smiled. "Oh wow, we love it here, don't we honey? We haven't had any problems until now. I can't believe this happened! It's such a peaceful neighborhood. That's part of why we moved in here."

Jordan seemed to agree. Then Johnson asked, "What time did you two get home today? We think the burglary was at, uh, around 11:00 this mornin.'" He looked at me and I nodded.

Fernando was relaxed but shifted in his chair between conversation beats. He looked down at the table often, and I wondered if the faint smell of marijuana I noticed by the living room was what made him uneasy. "We've been home all day. We just got back from vacation last night. Neither of us go back to work until Monday." He chuckled. "We were so tired, we came home last night and just collapsed. I didn't even take my darn shoes off! Needless to say, we slept in pretty late."

"Oh cool, where did you go on vacation?" I asked.

"We went to Rio de Janeiro, had a great time."

"What a fascinating place," Jordan added.

"We won't waste too much of your time," said Johnson. "What we really wanna know is if ya saw anything or heard anything. Was there a weird car, or did ya hear dogs barking or glass breakin'? Did you see Ms. Berkley? Any of your other neighbors home?"

The two looked at each other with frowns of dumbfounded ignorance. Fernando spoke first. "To be perfectly honest with you gentleman, we were out-and-about this morning, but I wasn't really paying attention. I think I remember seeing her car. Hon, can you think of anything?"

"Nothing out of the ordinary." Jordan had her hands clasped together on the table in front of her like she was negotiating the denuclearization of her sovereign nation. "We went to see Mr. Angelo across the street."

Johnson interrupted, his pen at the ready. "What time was that?"

"Um, it was earlier this morning."

"Yup, it was at 11:00," said Fernando, glancing at his gold designer watch. "We talked to him on his porch for an hour, mostly showed him pictures of our vacation."

"Why did you go see him?" I asked

He continued, "We asked him to take in our mail while we were gone the last two weeks and we came to get it back."

"It looked like there was still a lot out there," I said. But I looked around and saw a pregnant heap of magazines and envelopes on the dining room table, behind the kitchen, which was not visible from the entrance. "Oh, um never mind."

Jordan followed my gaze. "We get a lot of mail. We like magazines."

"Oh, and an hour later, I went back over to Angelo's. That was at 1 o'clock. He accidentally gave us a piece of mail. What a character. He looked like he was heading out," Fernando said.

I was about ready to move on to the next house, but I wanted to take advantage of the couple's forthcoming nature. "Angelo, has he lived here long?"

"Since before we moved in," responded Fernando. His demeanor had not changed, and he still seemed as willing to share information about his neighbors as he did about his vacation. "We like him, but he doesn't socialize much at all. He keeps to himself, he's a good neighbor, quiet."

Jordan added, "We try and talk to him when we see him. He lives by himself, so we figure he could use some company. I think he works from home. He hardly ever leaves the house."

"A real hermit crab!" interjected our friend with the gold watch.

Johnson was about ready to wrap it up too. "And did'ya notice any other neighbors home?"

"Old Mrs. McKraney was probably home, last house on the block. But everyone else would have been at work or school, I assume," Jordan said.

"And, we think the perp is someone who has been snooping around here before. Have you noticed anybody or anything out of place recently?"

After some stuttering, some mumbling, and some shaking of heads, they replied with a "no, not really," and a "not that I can think of."

Johnson closed his notepad and pushed his chair back, making it creak uncomfortably. "I think that'd be everthin' for now. Nate, anything else?"

"I think we are good to go." Before our hosts could stand, I added, "Actually, sorry, I do have one more question. "Were you two friendly with the house's previous owner, Ms. Berkley's grand-mother? Did you know her well?"

It caught them off guard in a way that it should not have. Under the table, Jordan's hand dropped to her hand husband's lap in a swift and subtle mo-tion. He squeezed her hand in return. By an almost imperceptible degree, her vertical posture gave way to the slightest of spinal curvatures caused by her shoulders moving forward half an inch. Fernando did not move in the least, sitting perfectly still, a large grin plastered unmovingly across his musta-chioed features. "No, no we didn't know her well," he said. "We saw her now and again. You know." He stood up, pulling Jordan up with him. "We're so very glad you're investigating this. It's just terri-ble. Sorry we couldn't be of more help."

Johnson rose as well, not seeming to have paid much attention to the closing exchange. I turned off my phone's camera and we left the house.

Outside, it only seemed to have become hotter,

even though the clouds had become thicker. Johnson looked around, adjusting his belt. "It's not gonna rain today is it?"

I shrugged, "I do not know."

"Where to next?"

I looked at the smallest house on the block, which was directly across from the one we were exiting; a car was in the drive. The house beside it was the one for sale, and that house sat facing Liza's new home. Behind them both was open grass, a modest tree line, and then the road from which we had driven. I pointed, "We go see Angelo. We know he was here this morning. He would be our best witness."

"Hrmph, well"—Johnson began walking—"I'm surprised he didn't come out when the flashin' lights showed up. D'ya think he could be your stalker/burglar?"

"Well if that couple is to be believed, (or Fernando anyway) we know he was home until at least 1 p.m. There is absolutely no way one person can tear up a house like that in under two hours. The carpet was torn up, the wallpaper was peeled back, and our guy even went into the attic, and I remember seeing some of the insulation ripped out.

Besides, if he had been listening in, knowing how long she would be gone, he would have taken all the time he could to search the place. Someone who was that committed and desperate to find something, wouldn't have subjected themselves to an hour of vacation photos on his porch."

"Fair enough. Speakin' of..."

We had arrived. It was a brown wood-frame house, the only one of such construction on the block. It was nice to look at but was a far cry from the perfectly trimmed lawn and meticulously decorated exterior of the house from which we had just come. Dark drapes obscured the house's innards at every window. There were no decorations or personal modifications of any kind. The only indication that anyone lived there at all was the fact that the lawn was freshly mowed and, as I said, there was a 90's era car parked out front.

We came up to the door, but it opened before Johnson could do what he called the "police pound." The man who opened it was a gruff, tired man in his forties, bald and pasty, with a large nose being his most prominent feature. He wore a gray sweatshirt with the sleeves cut off and basketball shorts flecked with dried paint. He also wore sandals, and his bare arms and legs looked like raw turkey left out to thaw. "What you need?" he asked.

"I'm Officer Johnson, this is Detective Nathan Gallup. There was a break-in next door, not too long ago. This mornin' actually. We were—"

"I saw nothing. I don't know nothing about it."

It was only then that I began to recognize what might have been an Eastern European accent. He looked at me, "Anything else? I'm busy."

"Your neighbors said they came and chatted with you this morning. Is that true?" I asked.

"Yes. Why?"

"And what time was that?" asked Johnson, looking at his notes.

"Did you see anything while you were out here? A car or anything?" I added.

"No, I told you, nothing. Everything was normal. I don't remember the time it was." I found it interesting that his words were filled with more apathy than impatience. The door was cracked open behind him now, his hand still on the knob.

I asked him, "Your neighbor Fernando said you

were getting ready to leave around 1:00, is that right?"

In the merest way, his stoic expression broke as his eyebrows lowered for an instant, almost knitting together before returning to their original positions. "Maybe. I went to dry-cleaners. Just came back." Feeling the conversation over, he turned to walk back inside.

"Sir," I took a step. "One last thing before we go. Have you seen or heard anything suspicious lately? Over the past month or two?"

He stopped. He looked me in the eye. He said nothing. He stepped inside. He said, "No." He closed the door.

"Friendly man," said Johnson.

As we walked back, we planned to visit the house on sale, then the two remaining houses. But as we walked closer to the house for sale, we spied an old lady across the street on the pavement in front of Liza's home, arguing with one of the officers whose job it was to secure the scene. "Dollars to donuts, that's Old Mrs. McKraney," grumbled Johnson.

"You sound like a cartoon character, Phil."

He chortled heartily as we changed our course

to meet with the woman. We overheard a piece of the conversation as we approached: "...is Ms. Berkley? Let me through! I have your badge number, and a very good memory, young lady!"

We stood for a few more seconds, watching the old woman rant emphatically. Then I approached her and said, "Hi, excuse me ma'am, hi. Liza is giving her statement right now, but she is just fine, no need to worry. Unfortunately, we cannot let you come any further, but forensics should be done soon, and then you can go in." The old woman turned from the officer who mouthed, *thank you* at me. "In the meantime, could we ask you a few questions?"

"But of course! This is, all of this, is nonsense, an outrage! Never in all my years of living here have we had one crime, especially not like this, in the middle of the day no less." She raised the metal cane on which she was leaning for emphasis. "It's these no-good politicians, is what it is sir. What hope is there for our community now? I do not... I no longer feel safe in my home."

And with that, her cane fell back to the ground, marking the end of her sermon. After a pause, she was clearly about to start up again until I interrupted her as quickly as I could. "Well, my name is Nathan Gallup, I am an investigator working for Liza. This is officer Johnson. We are asking the neighbors if they saw or heard anything suspicious today. Is it alright if I record our conversation?"

"Fine, fine." She waved her bony hand and continued. "It's about time someone came to speak with me. My name is Mary, Mary McKraney. I live at the house down there at the end of the road. I see everything that goes on around here. Oh, they don't think I notice what they do, but I notice all sorts of things. I walk my dog Polly every morning and evening. Dr. Henry says I need to walk, it's good for my hip. I see late-night visitors, arguments, all sorts of things. And do you know what? Just this morning, I'm glad one of you finally came to talk to me, because just this morning I saw someone stomping around in the woods, in the trees back there behind the house. I thought it was one of those teenagers from the high school again. But even then, I thought, this is too early for one of them. And I knew—"

"What time was this?" Johnson and I both asked at once. Johnson had his notebook out, but the woman was talking so fast, it was hard for him to keep up.

"Oh, well that was at 11:25 this morning. I started a little bit later today because Polly wasn't feeling well, but she ate and finally wanted to go on her walk. When George, that's my late husband, when he was still alive, he would walk Polly in the mornings. She never gave him any trouble. He would tell me about the teenagers and their shenanigans. They used to cause trouble, but nowadays, they are all inside with their phones and their desktops, so we don't see them as much."

"Can you give us a description?" I asked. "It looked like the burglar came in and left through the backdoor, so the person you described could very well be the burglar we are looking for."

"No, no," she said, "I'm afraid not. My eyesight is not what it was. I tried to see, but there was so much shade back there. It leads to swampland, you know. That's why the trees are so thick. You can be sure I'll watch out for Ms. Berkley though. When I have my prescriptions on, I can see the whole street from my top window."

"In that case," said Johnson, "have ya seen anything else the past couple months? We think the same guy who broke in might've been snoopin' around at night before."

"And committed mail fraud," I added. "Ms. Berkley has been receiving unmarked packages."

"Oh my! Well, I know nothing about that I'm afraid. I go to bed when the sun does. But you know, I remember earlier this year, my dear friend Hazel, bless her immortal soul, she received a package like that just before she passed. We were sitting in her kitchen when it came to the door."

"That's Liza's grandmother, right?"

"Oh, yes. I've known Liza since she was a little girl. She was always the cutest little thing, and so polite. Not like her mother, not at all. And Hazel, I met Hazel, even before she bought this house. She was an engineer like my husband. She and George worked together and back when she was still married, they would often come to our dinner parties."

"Was the package addressed to her?" I asked, with growing interest.

Mrs. McKraney leaned on her cane, trying to remember. "Yes, I believe it was. But there was no return address. I remember, she opened it, and it was a beautiful model airplane, silver and red. That was maybe a month before she passed. I came over for her apple pie recipe."

Johnson closed his notepad. "I'll need your written statement. It's no trouble. Just sign some papers and you can go."

"And Mrs. McKraney," I said, "can I have your phone number in case I have any follow-up questions?"

She leaned forward, using her cane as support, and poked me with her bony index finger. "Young man, if you have any more questions that can help end this dreadful business, you are to come to my door, and I'll make you my baked lasagna and some tea cakes. Understand?"

"Yes, ma'am."

"But not you," she said, turning to Johnson, "I won't have enough to feed you, sir."

That gave me quite a good laugh.

We went to the last two houses on the block. One of them had a messy assortment of children's toys on the lawn and was covered in decorations. We knocked, but no one seemed to be home. The place on sale was equally empty, and it looked permanently vacant. I took down the name and number of the real estate agent from its sign which stood out front. Then, we went into the grove behind the Berkley residence to have a look around, but found nothing except a lone boot print, stamped into a spot of mud.

A little while later, once the forensics team was finishing up and the sun was hanging lower in the sky, I took Johnson into the house where we met Liza and Sam in the kitchen. Sam asked, "Anything?"

I gave him the run-down. "We know someone was around back around 11:30. And we think, Liza, that your grandmother may have been receiving packages as well. Or at least one, not too long ago. Do you remember seeing a silver model plane?"

Liza, who was sitting at the table with her head in her hands, shook her head. "No."

"Okay, well, Sam, you can head back to the office, I'll find my own way back. Actually, on second thought, bag the elephant and bring it back here. Liza, if you can point out all the items you received in the mail, they will need to be handed in as evidence."

She slowly rose, her eyes red and puffy, and said nothing. Johnson and I followed her around, collecting the items. I took pictures for my own files (see attached) and tried not to say too much else, in case the cameras were still recording. When we were done, Sam came back with the elephant.

I handed it over to Johnson. "Last piece," I said. "I'll hear from you soon?"

He sniffed. "Yea-up. I'll call after I talk to the tech guys. Should be soon. But for now," he put out a meaty paw for me to shake, "gotta get back to it."

After he left, it was just me and Liza. And a big mess.

She sat down at the table again, looking exhausted. "Are you doing alright?" I asked, sitting next to her. I was never good at that sort of thing.

Her eyes teared up a little. "This is insane. I don't know if I can stay here."

"I know. I understand if you want to leave. But if you at least stay in Florida, I can, I *will* figure out who is doing this. But I might need you to do that. Okay?"

She nodded.

"Was anything stolen?" I asked.

"No, nothing. I don't think so. As far as I could tell, her jewelry and everything is still there. But a lot of stuff is broken, the picture frames, the TV. Ugh." She slumped down, burying her head in her arms.

"I know. It will be a lot with the insurance claims and the clean-up and all. Trust me, I know. But I just have a few more questions. Now, the bad news is, somebody was probably looking for something, and they may or may not have already found it. The good news is, I doubt you will be getting anymore packages, and it looks like it was just one guy who did all of this.

"The questions I need to ask you are about your grandmother. Based on what I have learned so far, it is worth exploring the possibility that the criminal may not have been targeting you, but rather, this has something to do with her. Or something she owned."

She sat up. "I don't know why; everyone loved her. Except my mother. Grandma wouldn't have deserved this," Liza said, gesturing around.

"And the couple next door? They acted strange when I mentioned her."

"I don't know them much at all. They weren't living here the last time I visited Grandma."

"I see. And Mrs. McKraney?"

Liza smiled with a set of teeth that either paid for a dentist's boat or put him out of a job. "She came to see me just before you came back. She's so sweet. I've known her my whole life. She said I could stay with her if I needed to, and to call if there's ever any trouble. She said she'd be watching day and night."

"And will you? Stay with her?"

Liza looked around. "I don't know. Maybe."

The sun was beginning to get ready for bed, and I stood up to turn on the light. "How soon after your grandmother's death did you move into the house?"

"It was right away, just after she passed, since I was already on my way down here to visit."

"Any particular reason?"

"No, I just hadn't seen her in a while and wanted to take a vacation."

I returned to my seat. "And she died of what?"

"It was sudden cardiac death. That's what the medical examiner said, anyway."

"Wait—the medical examiner? Did they do an autopsy?"

"Yes... they said the police found her under suspicious circumstances, and like I said, she was in perfect health, so I think they wanted to make sure it wasn't genetic or anything. That's all I know, I don't really remember anything, I'm sorry."

"No, no that's fine. I know you've been through a lot. Autopsies here are public record, and I can get ahold of the police report since I'm helping with your case. Was your grandmother working at the time? Mrs. McKraney said she was an engineer?"

"She had just retired, that's part of why I was coming to visit, to keep her company."

"And can you keep working? I know the burglar gutted your computer."

"I have everything backed up on servers, so yeah. I can report it to the insurance company too; I still have the serial numbers."

"Good." We sat quietly for a while as I mulled over the day's events. Then, partly thinking out loud, I reviewed: "Nothing has been stolen and someone has been recording us, either aurally, or visually as well. Whether you stay or not, I doubt our guy will come back anytime soon. He either has what he was looking for, or he thinks I will be watching which is why he made his move when he did. Our enemy is resourceful, patient, and very careful. However, before I know more about the situation, I do not feel comfortable recommending that you stay here. What do you want to do?"

Liza sighed, her head on the table, her yellow hair splayed about. "I'll stay with Mrs. McKraney until you catch him and until I can get the house cleaned up. Maybe it's more than one person though. Or not the same person."

"Maybe. But even if the person who sent the packages was different from the one who broke in, they are both nearby, and they are both working in concert. Anyway, you start packing and doing what you need to do, and I will set up my cameras. I can call the home-security lady and she can give you an estimate, maybe do the whole job tonight. She owes me a favor."

————————————

Later the next day, after I had gotten plenty of rest, I decided to start the next leg of my investigation with the realtor and the empty house directly across from Liza's. A chipper, high-pitched voice answered the phone when I called the real estate agent. I scheduled a tour of the open house for later that afternoon. If I had to, I could make it clear that it was for an investigation, but I did not want to be kept waiting and thought that a potential client would be treated more expeditiously. In the meantime, I went online to see what information I could find about the grandmother (Hazel Berkley) and her past.

Her social media pages were still active, and she had a modest presence. Mainly, she re-posted news of scientific discoveries and new technologies. Politically, she mostly leaned to the left, participating in different forms of activism, her chief concern being climate change, the topic about which she was most outspoken. Hazel was well liked online, and she had many friends. On her careers page, it said that she was a professor for about twenty years before receiving grants to do independent research. Finally, she began working in the research and development department of a company called Truskol Energy Corporation. She had two PhD's, one in nuclear physics and one in engineering, and she actively participated in online forums about those topics where she was referred to as "Dr. Berkley." I noticed that she shared information and traded advice often, from week to week, but abruptly stopped. I went back and cross referenced this with her work history and found that it took place right before she left her job. I jotted down the name of the energy corporation and a note underneath it to investigate the neighborhood's public property records. I put the notes on my keyboard and left to meet with the real estate agent. Sam came with me to check out the house and make sure nothing was amiss while I was across the street doing the tour.

"Hi there! Nate?" asked Patty the listing agent once I had arrived.

"That's me," I said.

She was a short, heavy woman with a clipboard, dark purple business suit, and a perfectly round afro. She handed me a packet of information. "Here is your buyer's packet, you can take a look at that as I show you around, and that should help you with your questions."

I followed her into the spacious home, watching as she carelessly put in the security code for the alarm. As we began, I looked for signs of a break-in or someone camping out to spy on Liza. I knew it was unlikely, but I wanted to cover my bases. The place was pristine, and nothing stood out, so as she talked, I began opening every closet and cabinet I could find.

"...as you can see, the full 2,400 square footage has..." I mostly tuned her out as she talked, nodding when appropriate.

Aside from the sinks and cabinets, there were no furnishings, which made my job easier. We went through a huge living area and a kitchen, past the back door, and were about to go upstairs. I stopped.

"Can we go through here?" I asked, pointing through the backdoor's window.

"Oh, you want to see the backyard? Absolutely. Just one sec." She took a key out of her pocket. "Oh!"

"What's wrong?"

"The door is already unlocked. I must've forgotten to lock it last time I did a showing."

Or someone knew the alarm code, I thought. "Do you do a lot of showings for this place?"

"Oh yes! We had an open house two weeks ago with good attendance, and I've done a private showing twice this year for the same man. So, there's a ton of interest, it's super, but no takers yet. It hasn't been on the market too long, and I expect it to sell soon."

We stepped outside, into the open backyard. I

walked around but saw no clear signs of anything suspicious. "And who contracted the house to be built? Why are they selling?"

"A sad story. The man who had this built was in a boating accident, and unfortunately can no longer live here. But it's truly an excellent property! As you can see, the backyard has plenty of room for..."

We went upstairs and I immediately moved to the front of the house, looking out of the bedroom windows. The largest room had the largest windows and a perfect view of Liza's house. At the widest window, I looked around and saw a ring of dirt on the floor. It looked like a partial footprint. Following the other patches of dirt around the room, I saw two more boot prints on the tile, clearer than the first. "Wow, this is beautiful tile." As I said this, I bent down with my miniature tapemeasure and pretended to gauge the tile's width. "Mind if I take a picture? I want to make sure the color matches some of my furniture."

"Not at all, please, be my guest."

I took a few pictures, leaving the tape measure on the floor. Once again, my instincts had paid off; the boot prints were the same size as the ones I found at Liza's break-in. I wanted to dust for prints at the window, but I needed to bring the issue to Johnson first so he could receive a warrant.

We finished with the tour, and I saw no further evidence of the intruder's presence. I bid Patty a fond farewell, telling her I would be in touch, and went across the street to meet back up with Sam.

"Liza came by," said Sam as I met up with him inside the truck.

"And?"

"And what?" he asked, munching on a candy bar.

"And what did she—where did you get that?"

He stopped eating the bar for a moment to look at it. "That nice old lady gave it to me. From up the street. She said I was doing God's work."

"Whatever that means. And she did not have one for me?"

An obvious look of guilt engulfed Sam's features but he said nothing. I grumbled and started up the truck, driving back to my comfortably worn armchair.

Once we arrived back at the office, I sat at my computer to do more research but found myself watching a movie instead. When one movie became two, I grabbed a snack from my desk. When two became three, I grabbed the bourbon. At that point, it was getting darker outside, and I needed my beauty sleep, so I decided to save some time and fall asleep right there in my chair.

After what felt like no time had passed, I was awoken abruptly by Sam who was shaking me. "Oh god, what do you *want*?"

"Nate, Mrs. McKraney called. She said she saw something!"

"Did I give her my number?"

"She said she saw someone 'prowling.'"

"What time is it, Sam? You should have gone home by now."

"I was finishing up the paperwork stuff for those divorce filings last week. I was on my way out when she called."

I groaned loud and long, unable to move or lift my head. "Did the cameras go off?"

"No."

"Alarm?"

"Nope."

"Do you want some more overtime?"

"Not really." After a pause, "What? Oh, come on, Nate. Linda's been complaining about me coming home late every week." I remained silent, knowing Sam would eventually cave. "Come on, Nate. That old lady talks forever!" After a moment of quiet during which Sam no doubt pondered his life choices, he noticed the empty bourbon container beside me and picked it up from my desk. "Ugh, fine. I'll stop there on my way home"—I gave him a thumbs-up—"but I'm not going next time."

"You said that last time," I said, but I think by then he had already left.

CHAPTER IV

THE YEAR 2076

The trio split up. At the jet, Nigel put his detector away and unrolled a bio-bag to take back to preserve the body. He also grabbed a cup of coffee from the pot. Still warm. He and Oslow drove back to the building where the grumpy-looking employees had begun filing out. He went inside and unzipped his coat, blowing his reddened nose on his sleeve. "Agh, Jesus." The harsh wind had stung his face, but the heat stung even more.

Doctor Jakobi was waiting by the body with two security guards.

"Alright doc. I need a stretcher or something so we can carry this guy outside."

"I'll see what I can do," said the doctor.

With the help of the two guards, large men with cultivated, serious expressions, Nigel placed the body in his bio bag and sealed it. They waited for Dr. Jakobi to return. "Where were you shmucks when this was going down?" Nigel asked, nodding toward the corpse.

The larger guard spoke. He sounded like an American. "We don't work when nobody's here. The place gets locked down for about four hours every day. If something's wrong, they call us to open the place back up."

"Then what was our friend here doing out back?"

The guard shrugged. "Maybe he got into some vodka. Maybe he was tweaking out on something. Look dude, we just keep the peace, make sure nothing gets stolen by the equator immigrants who mooch off the government site. And keep people out while the doors are open."

Doctor Jakobi came back with his stretcher. They loaded the body onto the snowmobile like they were sliding a turkey in the oven. Then, Nigel alone drove it back to his plane, almost losing his way in the blinding winter fury, only miraculously reached his destination.

He pressed a button on the side of the plane which slowly lowered a cargo port. He dumped Anton's enormity into its new home and shut the hold. He jumped inside the plane before his nose turned blue. Then, he made a call.

"Yo, Janice. It's me. Got a popsicle for you. Special delivery."

A woman with close-cut black hair in shiny tight curls appeared on the ship's monitor. "The Russian body? Wait, he is Russian right?"

Nigel pulled up Anton's file again. "Yes ma'am. Born and raised. I'll send the plane back and the body back. I need to keep digging here. Sending all the info and a piece of evidence onboard as well."

Janice sighed and began in a tone of mock annoyance "Not my department..."

"Jesus, will you just let them know? And make sure they send the plane *back* this time. I don't plan on camping out here."

She rolled her eyes. "Dammit, if you weren't so cute, I'd tell 'em to leave you down there."

"Then who would send you all those lovely dead bodies you spend all your time with? You would run out of friends."

"Hey, I get paid just like you. Speaking of which, I have work to do. Stop annoying me."

"Well I—" the screen went blank. "Well that was rude!" said Nigel to no one.

Begrudgingly, he sent his plane and its autopilot on its way and mounted the snowmobile once more.

Catherine was waiting outside the parking area when Nigel pulled up. It looked like everyone had gone back inside. Nigel dismounted and said, "Well howdy there Mrs. Supervisor!"

"Hello detective. I want to tell you; I talk to snow hydrologist about depth of knife. It was dropped much earlier, by day or so."

Nigel frowned. "Are you sure? It's really coming down."

"It looks like more snow because of wind. I assure you. We have computers for snowfall. Antarctica is still desert."

"Unless someone was stupid enough to try and hide it there." Nigel looked around at the endless expanse of snow and ice in every direction. "Nah. Well, if we can't trust you eggheads with numbers, we really are doomed, huh?"

Catherine smiled obligingly.

"Where's Oslow?" Nigel asked.

"Just inside. Do you want see him?"

"Uh, yeah. That's why I asked. By the way, how can I get one of those keycards or whatever to get in."

"I'm afraid, I cannot give one. I will have to let you in whenever you go to inside."

She let opened the door and Nigel stepped inside the wide, circular room once more. Everyone was avoiding eye contact now that the body was gone, probably to avoid questioning and to look as innocent as possible. Everyone except Oslow, that is.

Nigel walked over to him. "Oz, my boy. Quick question. I know you got a good 200 or so people here, but can you think of any who are big? Like really big, muscular six-foot-ten type dudes?"

"Let me think. Well, our security guards are very large. Other than that, maybe one or two, but I couldn't think of their names. I will try."

"Well, thanks for nothin,' Oz. If someone else dies before I catch this guy, it's on you." Nigel said it jokingly, but Oslow seemed legitimately dejected. Nigel looked around, but Carl was nowhere to be seen. He gave Oslow a rough pat on the shoulder and walked past him saying, "I'll go talk to the roomie. You gonna show me where that is?"

"Yes, I can do that. I'll take you right there."

The electric snowmobile was started up, and as they rode, the storm began to lessen its fury. The darkness however did not abate. "When's morning?" asked Nigel.

"It will not be light for another nineteen hours at least."

"Of course it won't."

In no time, they approached the outskirts of the tightly packed housing units, each unit no more than ten and a half feet tall. A sense of claustrophobia pervaded the area, no doubt a byproduct of trying to stave off the cold. A general din rose above the wind, mixing with the sound of the storm to create an eerie whisper. They parked the mobile in its designated spot and stepped toward the unconventional looking village. They started moving in between shelter units, most for housing, some, set up as trading posts and stores. Nigel felt immensely uncomfortable looking left and right, as perfectly parallel rows and rows of cubes disappeared into the thick gray dark on either side. He noticed that each shelter was numbered with a thick black stenciled numeral. The unit next to him read *67* and it smelled of fish.

No one seemed to pay the pair any mind as residents ate under heat lamps or futilely tried to shovel their housing units out from under a flood of snow. In between the buildings, people walked slowly up and down, unintentionally cementing a dangerous looking and icy pathway. It was hedged in on either side by piles of snow which were over four feet high in some areas of the less frequented avenues.

As the two walked, Nigel could hear a confluence of several languages, many of Spanish origin. After navigating a slippery path, they arrived at a unit marked *58*. "We are here," said Oslow.

Nigel looked around outside the unit while Oslow knocked, spoke with someone in Russian, then entered the structure. After a moment, a man emerged with Oslow. The shriveled raisin of a man in thick furs surprised Nigel. In an era when it was common for humans to live well into their 120s, remaining independent even into their latest years, Nigel was still surprised to see someone so old, so far south. The elderly held on to their dignity and property as long as they could, until they were inevitably driven from their homes by increasing climate swings and full-scale economic collapses.

"And who might you be?" Nigel asked. The man looked gruff and tired. He had a pale face, deeply lined by too many troubles, and a nose so large it took up almost half his face. Underneath lay a white moustache and beard so bushy, it disappeared his skinny neck, growing yellow at the edges. Even under all his fur, his gaunt and withered frame was clearly evident, and Nigel was afraid that if left out in the sun too long, he would continue to shrivel, then disappear.

"Alexi," said Alexi. I understand there's been murder?"

His English was good, so good, that Nigel wondered whether English or Russian was his first language. "Yes, there was. Anton, the big man. You were friends?"

"I didn't know him long," Alexi rasped.

"That's not much of an answer, Alex."

"*Alexi.* We were friendly."

"I see. Well, I'm gonna need to have a look inside. Since this is government property, I have all the permission I need."

"Go right ahead" said the old man. "His stuff is there."

His "stuff" was not much. There were two beds only a few feet apart. One side was swept, and had no clutter, while the other was overloaded with clothes and gear. Many boxes and trunks hung from a net attached to the ceiling above the beds. There were also some low shelves, and more boxes, and some pairs of shoes underneath both beds. A single gray trunk the size of a small table sat between the low mattresses, straight through to the back of the room.

And that was it. No windows, no bathroom, no kitchen. The entire unit was one room, and everyone seemed to live communally, sharing latrines and bonfires alike. Nigel had his little robot scan the unit, then Oslow came in to oversee.

"I assume this is Anton's side," Nigel said, pointing to a pair of boots fit only for a yeti.

"Yes. Alexi keeps everything tidy," said Oslow.

Nigel tossed the place, searching through every one of Anton's belonging that he could find. Unlike Alexi, or anyone else on the planet, Anton had no phone, head visor, personal computer, or wearables anywhere to be found. But he also had no

books, paper, photos of his wife, or anything to oc-
cupy his free time, making it unlikely that he had
no electronics to begin with. Even if the murderer
stole what Anton had on him, reasoned Nigel,
would he or she have had time to double back and
steal from his home?

"Yo Ozzy, get the old guy in here." Alexi entered, seemingly unfazed by the mess Nigel had
made. "Were you here a day ago when this was
going down?" Nigel asked, looking at Oslow who
stood anxiously in the doorway.

"At 1:00 to 5:00 a.m.," offered Oslow helpfully.
"While the center was closed."

"Sorry gentleman, I would've been asleep. I am
a heavy sleeper."

"I'm sure you are," said Nigel, "but the man
weighed three hundred pounds and slept right
next to you. Was he here when you went to sleep?"

"I'm not sure. I don't think so. He might have
already left."

"Where was he going? The building was locked
down."

Alexi sat down slowly on his bed. "I don't
know. He didn't tell me."

Nigel sighed. "So, you were the closest person

to him, you were here that night, and yet he never spoke about anything he was doing, and you know nothing. DO I have that right?"

"It looks that way," said Alexi disappointedly.

"Right, well, what did he do in his free time? Any drinking, gambling, fight clubs? Anybody he didn't like, owed money to?"

"He liked vodka." Alexi stood slowly and with effort, then walked over to the wall above Anton's bed and banged on it twice with the side of his fist. A panel opened, filled with half a dozen bottles of alcohol.

"That's handy." Nigel took a moment to have his digitizer scan the bottles' prints. "But I don't think he broke his neck drinking."

"Maybe he owed somebody money for them," Alexi offered, sitting down again.

"Is that what you think happened?"

"I don't know."

"Of course, you don't. Why would you know anything that might be useful?" Nigel put some of Anton's belongings back where he had found them. "Why are you here anyway? Don't see a lot of old-timers down here."

"Better the cold than the heat at my age. Besides, it's better to come now than in ten years when half the ice has melted away and coming here will be a luxury most people can't afford."

"You're smarter than you look old-timer."

"That's what they tell me. Now, if you're done, I was getting ready for my nap."

"Back to it then," said Nigel. "And watch your neck."

Oslow and Nigel exited the domicile. They split up to canvas the shelter quadrant, hoping to find out what Anton was doing and why he had left. Nigel met with as many residents as possible, all of whom knew Anton, but only in passing. None knew him as more than an acquaintance, despite his having been there almost a year.

"I got 2 a.m.," Nigel reported after he and Oslow found each other once more.

"The same for me, detective. He left from in between these buildings here at that time. But most people were asleep, so not many saw him."

"Any clue what he was doing? Wasn't it snowing by then?"

"Yes. No one knew where he was going, but as a maintenance worker, he was always on call."

"So, whoever could call him in might have led him out there?"

"Maybe. But that's anyone who works in the buildings."

"Then back to the buildings we go. Sally forth, driver!"

The pair drove off, back whence their quest began.

"By the way," Nigel said leaning over so Oslow could hear him over the wind. "Did you call the wife yet?"

Oslow kept his eyes ahead, on the dim lights which twinkled through the flurry of white gray. "I think Supervisor Catherine called right after she called the UN. Or somebody did, I'm sure." There was a ringing noise and Oslow toggled something on his arm. "Speaking of the Supervisor, she has the list ready that you asked for."

"Well tell her to send it through already." Shortly after these words were spoken, Nigel received an alert on the backside of his glove. He patched the file through to his main computer system. "And the people you talked to. Did they say if Anton had any computers or anything that he used? You didn't forget, did you?"

Oslow thought a moment. "Oh right, yes I did ask. A couple people said he always wore earbuds when he was out, so it was hard for people to talk to him. And I myself remember he had an old machine, a $2 laptop that I remember was on his bed when we assigned Alexi to his quarters and I had to explain it was only temporary. That was maybe a month ago."

"Was he really upset about it?"

"No, not at all, he knew his wife would be away a while and I assured him that Alexi would be reassigned before she came back."

"When was she supposed to come back?"

"I'm not sure. Very soon, I think."

"And how long has Alexi been here?"

"Much longer, a few years maybe?"

"Why was he moved?"

"Catherine told me of a zoning issue with a large family and Alexi graciously agreed to be relocated."

Nigel remained silent, considering the possibilities. He also considered what he might be forced to eat for dinner.

CHAPTER V

THE YEAR 2016

The next morning, before Sam or any sane and reasonable people had gone into work, I went down the street for a bagel. While waiting in line, I called Johnson who I knew would be on duty. "Hey, Phil."

"Mornin' Nate."

"I found a boot print. It was in the empty house."

"Okay."

"And I sent in an autopsy report request last night for the grandmother. Liza says it was natural causes, but the autopsy was done because of suspicious circumstances. Do you think you could get the police report for me? Hazel Berkley, same spelling as the granddaughter."

"That should be doable. I can tell you the info or hand it to you in person. You're officially hired on this as of this morning."

"And the cameras?" I asked, receiving my everything bagel and coffee in a white paper bag.

"Right, right, right. They were all definitely cameras. I'll have more info for you later on. S'all I got right now."

"Thanks, I think I will come by the station today for that report."

"Oh-kay, gottta go."

"Bye." I hung up and walked back to my office to finish up my research from the day before, starting with the company, Truskol. I was able to find a great deal of information about it through my own means, as there was surprisingly little information about it publicly. Publicly, it was a Russian-based company that had been doing business in the US since 1992. The company was involved in manufacturing and exporting various forms of traditional and renewable energy and had started looking for a competitive edge in recent years by developing more efficient sources of renewable energy.

Investigating financial information from the Secretary of State's office, I looked through Truskol's revenue history, and eventually noticed that the company seemed to be heavily funded by the Russian government. I printed out a list of all current and former employees, executives, owners, and pension and benefit filings. It was around that time that Sam walked in, the door to my office having been left open.

"You look like you got plenty of sleep," Sam said grumpily.

"Did she have anything useful?"

"No. It was just some guy going door to door with pictures of his missing cat. I asked her neighbor. Didn't stop her talking my ear off though!"

"Wait, which neighbor?"

"The lady in the house next door. With the kids. Her name was"—Sam scrolled through his phone—"Cassandra."

"Well thanks anyway, Sam. I appreciate it. Since you're here, can you pull up the neighborhood's property records? I need to go down to the station."

"Are they cooperating? You're investigating it anyway."

"Yup, I am now officially on the case."

———————————————

After a shower at my apartment, I was at the precinct, but Johnson was out, so I had to wait by the entrance as noisy people and noisy cops walked by. I did some more research about Truskol on my phone. Their company also had a hand in the maintenance of some nuclear power reactors around Russia. After I saved the company's Florida address to my phone, I did some research on Liza. Like me, she had little presence online, and what she did have was mostly professional. All I really learned was that she had been doing graphic design since college and was once a girl scout. I found nothing that stood out, and put a pin in it, convinced that the situation had less to do with her than it did with Hazel.

After a while, I began to grow impatient with Johnson but was told he would soon return. A couple of plainclothes detectives walked by whom I recognized, and they nodded in my direction. But once I saw who was walking behind them, I made a noise of audible discomfort.

"Nate. What are you doing here?" asked a short man with a rusty beard, a few wrinkles, and a forceful disposition. He smelled of cigarettes and spite.

"Chief." I remained seated.

"Who you waiting for? You're doing that break-in or whatever it was, aren't you?"

"Yes."

"How the mighty have fallen. I haven't seen you around here in a while."

"You haven't called."

He adjusted his belt and straightened his posture. "I approved you for this didn't I? Anyway, I oughta be off. I'm the chief. Lots of chiefly things to do."

"Goodbye."

"By the way, you have something on your shoe." And with that, he walked off.

I looked at the shoe in question, attached to the ankle that was propped up on my knee in a gentlemanly fashion. "Aw crap." I took a pen from my pocket and began scraping the gum out from its nestled home in my tread.

"Whatcha doin' there?" Johnson approached, a smile on his face and a file in his hands.

"Good morning. I see you had your breakfast."

"Huh? Oh." He brushed the crumbs from his shirt. "Here's a copy of the incident report. Looks like the neighbor called it in. McKraney."

I took a look. There was a lot of information to parse through, so I let Johnson go back to work. In essence, the day Hazel died, the door to the house was left open, some of the furniture was knocked over, there was relatively new, but vague bruising on the arms, and, as Liza had said, Hazel's medical history showed no sign of any significant illness or heart disease. To be honest, I was surprised they did an autopsy at all, but I was glad to see that they were being thorough. She was 76 years old at the time.

"Here you go," I said, handing Johnson back the file when I had finished. He was sitting at his desk, surrounded by the raucous clamor of justice in action. The desk was too small for him, his arm taking up a third the real estate. "I talked to Henry," I said.

"I still can't believe they made him chief. Shame you didn't stick around."

"Yeah, yeah, I have heard it all before."

"Anythin' useful in there?" he asked, gesturing toward the file on his miniature desk.

"I do not know. Maybe. My client says she never saw that model airplane, and the door *was* open."

"Well, you know where to find me. I'll be callin' you about those cameras soon. In the meantime," he gestured toward the desk.

"Sure, Phil. Back to the grind." I gave him a pat on the back and went on my way. Exiting the precinct, I decided to start up the Nate-mobile and drive to Hazel's old workplace to talk to some of her coworkers. The main offices stood in front of, what was either a storage building, or a small manufacturing facility.

As I drove closer, it seemed strange that there were so few cars in the parking lot during the workweek. Taking this into consideration, I parked two blocks away and walked back to the building. There was a large dumpster out front filled with everything that belonged in an office. *Uh oh.* I walked inside and the place was completely empty. The entire first floor was stripped bare. Based on the discoloration of the floor, I could see where there was once a reception area and next to it, a security check station. Further back, four elevators stood silent. They required some sort of badge or key to operate. Likewise, the entrance to the staircase was open, but the door to the second floor required a similar method of activation.

I left the office and went around back toward the domed warehouse-type building. The first door I tried was locked, and the only windows were either on the roof, or all the way at the top of the huge structure. The sun's heat was blazing straight down upon the asphalt, unfiltered, unadulterated, and unchallenged by neither cloud nor structure, and the asphalt in its turn reflected what it could back toward me. Alone in such an expanse of heated emptiness, I was given the uncomfortable feeling of being the key ingredient in the preparation of someone's omelet.

Then, I swear, out of absolutely nowhere, a woman approached with two men in security guard uniforms. She was thin and stern. The other two were not so thin but just as stern. "Can I help you?" she asked in a tone that made her seem like a person who would not be very helpful.

"Hi, yes. I was led to believe this was the Tampa office for Truskol Energy Corporation."

"It was, now it is not."

"You guys closed? It was not on your website."

"Yes, this office has closed."

"What happened?" She stood far enough away that I had to raise my voice a little, and it echoed off the two buildings.

"If you have any questions, you can call the main office at the number on the website."

"Like, was it a funding issue, or like, because I was looking to invest—"

"Please leave," she said raising her bony arm and pointing toward the street. The security guards both took a step forward.

"Okay, okay," I am leaving.

Disappointed, I walked back to my truck and pulled the stack of paper I had printed off, out of the glove compartment. The list of employees at the company was not short, and before I started trying to dig any further into them, I remembered that I already knew of someone Hazel had worked with at the company. And I was pretty hungry.

CHAPTER VI

THE YEAR 2016

I drove back to the neighborhood. Old Mrs. McKraney was sitting on her porch in a wide basket chair, knitting. Her dog Polly started yapping as I approached and ran around me excitedly, jumping on its hind legs, until Mrs. McKraney stamped her cane on the wooden boards and called it back into the house. The dog bowed its head and reluctantly sulked back inside after the second command. I noticed that Mrs. McKraney had left the front door open, with not even the screen door as protection. That was odd, I thought, considering the circumstances. She said, "Well hello again detective," as I continued walking up the driveway.

"Hi there, Mrs. McKraney."

"Staying for some lasagna? Your friend last night refused to stay! I was in a distressed state, and all he could think about was leaving. Now, I admit it was very late. But that's the problem these days, everyone is always in a rush, always trying to be somewhere, but once they're there, they need to be someplace else. Liza says you're a sensible young man, does that make any sense to you?"

"No ma'am, it does not." I was on the porch now.

"Well?"

"Um..."

"You won't refuse an old lady's hospitality, will you? You're staying for lunch?"

"Oh! Yes, I think I will."

"Good." She put aside her knitting and rose, with both my assistance and that of her cane. She grabbed my arm and led me into her kitchen. "Liza should be back in time to join us. You know, you're such a handsome young man. Although you could do to lose some of that stubble." At this, I laughed in a guffawing sort of way. She did not seem to notice my reaction as she began preparing ingredients. "I don't know why men think they needn't put effort into their appearance. We women must do so much. Anyway, Liza seems to respect you. You won't disappoint her, will you?"

"I will try my best. I think, with your help, I can find this guy."

"Good, good," she said. "Handsome young men so often disappoint."

"Well, maybe you can help me. I was wondering if you could tell me a little about your husband George's work. What were the kinds of things he worked on with Hazel?"

"I'm afraid, most of that gobbledygook was beyond me. He stopped trying a long time ago, trying to explain his work to me. But that's not very helpful, is it? From what I understood, he was doing nuclear research. But he promised me he wasn't making bombs. I made him promise. He was working for that, for the energy company... oh, what was its name?"

"Truskol?"

"Yes, that's the one." She began pouring sauce. "He started working there just after they opened. He started working with Hazel a bit after that. She kept working there, but he retired in, hmm, five years ago, now. Can you believe how quickly the time goes? It could've been just yesterday. He worked there for nineteen years. I never worked, myself. Not professionally anyway. Somebody had to raise our three beautiful children."

"Is this them?" I asked, picking up a photo.

"Hm? Oh yes, my beautiful boys, all men now. Oh shoot!" She dropped a can, and I bent down to pick it up for her.

"Do they live around here?"

"Oh no, they couldn't stay to keep their tirelessly loving mother company. They had to go off across the country. Now I hardly see them. My youngest is in Buffalo, that's Larry, then Frank is in Baltimore, he gave me two perfect grandbabies, and Chris is in Canada right now with his new wife, but he should be coming back soon. There's nothing worse than breaking your mother's heart. You didn't abandon your mamma, did you?"

"It was more the other way around."

"Ah. Well, in any case, you turned out alright, didn't you?"

"I suppose I did."

"The lasagna should be ready in about an hour. It's an old family recipe. The secret is the ricotta cheese on, top like this. And of course, only the freshest ingredients. My great grandmomma taught me how to make this when I was a little girl." She turned toward me, pointing down the hall. "If you want, while you wait, you can look through George's work papers. My sons moved them all up to the attic from his study. You can root around in there all you want. I never go up there anymore anyway, what with my hip and all. I have not the spryness of youth, as they say."

She led me across creaky floors and shuttered rooms filled with dust and memories, to an open attic with a wooden ladder already extended. She gave me some parting advice, and the tapping of her cane slowly faded out of earshot as she hurried back to her meal preparations. I climbed the dusty ladder which creaked angrily. The attic was almost the length of the entire house. A terribly small window caked in dust on the other side of the attic afforded almost no light, and I sought the dangling pull switch Mrs. McKraney had described before we parted. It helped. I moved slowly, so as not to stir up too much dust. The attic had to have been filled with more belongings than the rest of the house, and I had a hard time making my way through the chaotic collection of storage containers, bags, clothing, furniture, and holiday decorations.

Finally, I came across the collection of boxes Mrs. McKraney described. A handful were marked "George" or "'76." It was disorganized, but most of the papers and notebooks were separate from his other possessions. The sheer number of them made me anxious, and I did not want to spend the rest of the week in that woman's home, accommodating as she was. I dove straight in, looking for the more recent paperwork that might include mention of Hazel. To my surprise, it looked like they collaborated often, and before he retired, George was helping her construct an insanely complex-looking device or set of devices. I skimmed most of it, taking pictures of everything that looked useful. Although truthfully, I had very little idea what that was. It seemed like he had kept working with Hazel after he retired, but I could only tell by the handwriting.

Hidden in the Truskol paperwork was a small collection of photographs from different years at the company. Luckily for me, the names of the employees pictured were written on the backs of them. I glanced at them each, but one picture stuck out to me more than the others. It had a young man, no more than twenty, standing next to George, whom I recognized from photographs around the home. The back read:

December 1992

One Year Anniversary

Underneath was a list of names that referenced the people in the photo from left to right. There were ten people in the photo, probably department heads. What had stuck out to me was how vaguely familiar the young man looked. But I had no idea who he was, only a feeling. The name on the back read, *Rurik Kuznetsov.*

"Nate!" The voice came from downstairs. It sounded like Liza. "Food!"

Aside from the pictures and a few of Hazel's notes, the attic trip did not seem to be getting me anywhere, so I packed everything up and tiptoed back to the attic ladder, careful not to disturb the dust mites. Immediately, the intoxicating aroma of fresh pasta which now permeated the house, overcame my senses, and my stomach perceptibly rumbled. In the kitchen, Liza was pulling the lasagna out of the oven and Mrs. McKraney was setting the table. I felt very special indeed. But as often happens, I knew it would only make me feel guilty if I failed to catch Liza's stalker.

Mrs. McKraney caught me eyeing the steaming lasagna. "I've seen that look before. When's the last time you had a home-cooked meal?"

"Don't ask me that. Then I would be forced to answer."

Liza smiled and shook her head. Mrs. McKraney continued. "Nobody to cook for you? I find that hard to believe."

In the reflection of the teakettle, I caught her giving Liza a wink, which left me decidedly uncomfortable. But my hunger and the need to extract more answers to new questions, kept me where I was, and I took a seat at the table. I texted Sam to let him know I would be late coming back, and he sent the street's property records list in return. Liza sat across from me at the table, and Mrs. McKraney joined us, sitting next to me. She had us hold hands to say the blessing, after a tired and futile objection from Liza, who smiled at me, apologizing with her eyes. It was good to see my client in better spirits than she had been the day before, but I knew a lot of it had to do with her trust in me to finish the thing. I stared at the table.

As soon as we began to dig in, Mrs. McKraney started up again, asking, "Did you find anything up there? You know my boys put all of that up there, so I don't know where anything is. I haven't been up there in ages. You know, what with my hip and—"

"What were you looking for?" asked Liza.

"For now, I am still entertaining the idea that this had more to do with Hazel's house than with you, Liza. I wanted to learn more about your grandmother's coworkers and her work, and I knew the late Mr. McKraney worked with her for a long time."

"He did," Liza nodded, rubbing her temples.

"Oh, do call him George," Mrs. McKraney said, lobbing a heaping slice of lasagna onto her plate. "He hated when people called him 'Mr. McKraney.' Had to do with his father. That was a vile man, in his whole life, he did more smoking than talking."

"Yes, well, I found a lot, but also not much. Mostly notes. Liza, did your grandmother keep any notes from her work? Did she ever bring work home?"

"I didn't see any when I moved in. I went

through all her files and her desks, but it was all bills and insurance paperwork."

I thought about this for a moment. "I find that extremely interesting. It could have been what our stalker friend was after. It seemed like she was doing some high-level work. Although why he would need cameras..."

Mrs. McKraney jumped in, having somehow eaten half her helping of lasagna and greens already. "You know what you should do, you could try visiting where she worked. See if anyone there knew what she was up to. I'm sure I have the address written down around here somewhere. I can never find anything anymore. You can probably find it in George's paperwork."

"Actually, I meant to bring that up. The place is closed, at least that office is. I went by there today."

"Closed? I don't believe it. It's probably all these taxes the governor keeps pushing through. How are you supposed to run a business?"

"Everything was cleared out," I added.

"But why?"

Liza said, "I wonder if they're moving buildings."

"It didn't seem like it. But I certainly intend to find out. This lasagna is delicious by the way."

"Yes, thank you Mrs. McKraney, it's very good."

"Isn't it?" Mrs. McKraney was already heaping more food on her plate. The next mystery I had to solve was where she put it all. "My great grand-momma invented the recipe herself. I invite the neighbors to dinner all the time, don't I Liza? A few times a month. But do they ever come? Cassandra and the girls from next door come by every now and then. But that couple that bought the Patterson's old house—"

"Jordan and Fernando?" I asked.

"Yes, them. They've never come over. And the last time I baked them lasagna, they never returned my dish! What kind of uncivilized barbarians don't return a dish?" Her voice was becoming louder and shriller.

"I take it you do *not* like them," I stated questioningly.

"A pair of troublemakers they are. I don't trust them. They can't come by to visit an old widow, but they have plenty of visitors, all hours of the night, when civilized people should be asleep. At least Angelo has the decency to return a dish. Even back when they moved in, I didn't like them. They were always bothering Hazel with something or other, and they always wait too long to mow their lawn."

"I thought they seemed friendly enough when I interviewed them." I offered.

Liza chimed in, absentmindedly playing with the last bit of food on her plate, obviously not planning to eat it. "They did act kind of strange when I first moved in. They said they were friends with my grandma and asked me a lot of really personal questions."

"Like what?" I asked.

"Stuff like, about my relationship with Grandma and where I had been, why I didn't visit more often. I don't know, it was just kind of weird. Now that I think about it, I kind of remember them asking whether I knew where she worked, too. But that was only after the funeral. They didn't say anything to me before then. I don't think they even stayed for the whole service."

There was a pause as Mrs. McKraney finished her second helping of lasagna. Then she said, "Well, you know how Hazel was, she always saw the good in people, she was always friendly with them. I, on the other hand, never cared for them at all. And, how was it they didn't hear the break-in next door when she died? They couldn't have heard or seen something wrong and gone to see if they could help? And the break-in the other day. They were home for that, yet they heard nothing?"

"You think it was a break-in that day?" I asked.

"It had to be. As trusting as Hazel was, she never would have left the door open like that, walking halfway through her house. On hot days or at night, I like to leave the door open sometimes, you know, it's quiet around here. Every time I did, Hazel would lecture me endlessly about the price of air conditioning, mosquitos, burglars, any other nonsense she could think of. And she would accept none of that at her house."

"That is interesting. But let me just say, I am so sorry you had to deal with that. Finding her, I mean. I have been there before and know it is a shocking experience. But let me ask, was there anything else that seemed strange to you? It could be important."

"Of course! As soon as I came to the house, I knew something was wrong. Her chairs were all knocked over and the carpet was muddy. She never wore shoes in the house."

"And she wasn't wearing shoes?" asked Liza.

"No, of course not."

That means she did not just run into the house with chest pains. The door was left open after she took her shoes off. "Well please, if either of you think of anything else about her that might cause someone to want something valuable of hers or to want something from her, please let me know. I want to entertain this hypothesis a little while longer."

————————————

Later, I helped clear the dishes and offered to help wash, even though I was still technically on the job and it was the middle of the workday. (Free lasagna is the best part of being your own boss). My offer to help was soundly rejected by the widow McKraney, and I was instructed to stay until she wrapped up the rest of the lasagna for me to take home.

Liza went to the bathroom, and I went out onto the porch to take a break from Mrs. McKraney for a few minutes. I leaned on the rail—the sun still shining down with ferocious determination—and scrolled through some of the photos I had taken in the attic. I knew I would need a scientist to help me understand what most of the papers were referencing, and I might track down one of Hazel's American coworkers at some point. I tried to absorb all the new information I had learned over the past few hours. Since Liza barged into my office, I had been presented with a nonstop series of coincidences and escalating circumstances that were beginning to make me concerned for the safety of my client.

Phone in hand, I took a minute to glance at the property records Sam had sent me. Fernando and Jordan had indeed bought their house the year before. The empty house had indeed been newly constructed. Mrs. McKraney was indeed old as dirt. Hazel bought her house in 1993 from a man named Mikkal Lang. That would have made Liza about five years old at the time. The timelines seemed to track.

After ten minutes or so, Liza walked out and joined me on the porch, carrying a dish. She had changed into less professional clothing, more appropriate for the climate. "Here you go, Nate. Special delivery." She laid the dish on the banister by my arm.

"Just so you know," I replied, "this dish does not count as payment for my services."

She laughed, joining me at the banister, to look out at the row of houses.

I patted my stomach, "I have to say, that was truly delicious lasagna. Really, the food was peerless."

"There's more for desert if you want to stick around."

"Perhaps," I said, stroking the stubble on my chin. "How has everything been going, with the insurance and all that?"

"Honestly, it's been a pain in the ass. I might have to drop a project to deal with all this." She smelled of strawberries. And lasagna.

"Hopefully I can give you some peace of mind. I feel close finding this guy, but I still have no working theory. Not yet."

"No offense, but it seems like you're always working. Do you ever take a break? Not that I'm complaining." She smiled.

"This guy could be really dangerous. Believe it or not, it is not often I get a case like this."

She leaned closer, half her golden hair falling in

front of her face. "So, what you're saying is, I'm a special case?"

"Well, I—" My phone rang. It was Johnson. "Sorry Liza, this is about the case."

"By all means." She sat in a wicker chair at the end of the porch.

"Go for Nate," I said, answering the phone.

"What's that?" asked Johnson.

"What?"

"That! 'Go for Nate.' When didya start doin' that?"

"I don... I was just trying it out. I thought it would sound cool, you know, shorten the pleasantries." Out of the corner of my eye, I could see Liza smirking. "Anyway, what do you have for me?"

"Okay, Phil is going."

"What? Where are you going? Oh wait. Just, ugh."

Johnson snickered, clearly amused with himself. "Tech took a look at them hidden cams. The first three were transmitting live, but they could only transmit from a short range. From that house, it would have to have been one of the neighbors."

"Or the woods, right?" I asked.

"Maybe, but not far in. I don't know how in the hell that would work though. But if you wanna check the trees for power outlets, be my guest."

"What about the other ones?"

"Uh, yeah so, the rest are a different type of camera, tech guys have never seen it before, maybe foreign or kit bashed. They last, er, not quite as long, but still an upgrade. Smaller, less power, and more range."

"What are we talking?"

"About county limits, give or take a few blocks."

"Can you track the signal?"

"All of 'em had a kill switch. They were shut down remotely."

"Anything else?"

"Not right now. Wait, hold on, I forgot. We thought we had no prints, but we got a full set from the bathroom. Looks like the guy took his glove off to pee. I'll call back if they get the model of those last three cameras. I'll email you all the numbers and everythin.'"

"Thanks." I hung up and paced along the boards of the porch's floor, absentmindedly tapping my chin with the edge of the phone.

Liza broke my reverie after an indulgent amount of time. "Well?" For a minute, I had forgotten she was there.

"The um," I continued to pace. "The cameras were short range. That face you saw; did he have a moustache by any chance?"

"I don't think so. I'm not really sure."

I grabbed my leftovers and jumped down from the porch during Liza's response. "I think I have to pay a trip to your next-door neighbors." She stood up as I kept walking toward my truck. I hollered, "Tell Mrs. McKraney goodbye for me and thanks for the pasta." As I threw the dish in my truck, I decided to walk to Fernando and Jordan's house, making it easier to catch them off guard.

CHAPTER VII

THE YEAR 2076

Back at the main research station, Oslow let the detective in through the side entrance. Nigel strolled around for a bit, watching all the researchers hard at work doing math and other complicated things. Or, at least, that is what he assumed they were doing. Some of them had unseen workspaces visible only to the people using them. Others were scribbling down notes, arguing, or just mindlessly watching monitors that had incomprehensible networks of dots and lines blinking different patterns every few seconds. One room was entirely dedicated to an enormous 3D rendering of a side of the Antarctic continent, its surfaces and weather patterns color-coded and constantly shifting. Nigel enjoyed that room.

Upstairs, he put his feet up in a cozy lounge area which thankfully included a pot of coffee. He went over some of his notes on the case, then skimmed through the list of employees and residents. They were long lists. He yawned.

A livid-sounding voice boomed from the entrance behind Nigel. "Is this what you get paid to do? You came all the way to Antarctica just to skive off and sit around?"

Nigel turned. "Hey, it's, um, turtleneck-man."

"Carl," he said, crossing his arms as aggressively as possible.

"Yeah, right. Let me find you in this list here." Nigel returned his attention to the tablet he held. "Wow looks like you're the only Carl, Carl. Congrats. Carl. Or maybe I should call you Dr. Carl, all these fancy degrees. Says you're in charge of snow. How impressive."

Carl's face was red. "Look, you pre—"

Nigel remained seated but turned off the tablet he was using in order to sip his coffee with two hands. "You seem extremely interested with this case. What was a lowly janitor to you?"

Carl turned purple. "He was not a janitor! Look, I hardly knew the bloke, but people respected him around here. He was a mechanical engineer, he kept things running. If we keep losing guys like that, we'll all freeze to death."

"You think it'll keep happening?"

"N-no, I don't... just catch the piece of shite who did this!"

"That's what I'm doing."

"Well it looks like what you're doing is sitting on your arse while some gutter filth is slaughtering scientists that are this world's best chance for survival! So yeah, I'd say I'm kinda interested in the investigation."

"Sounds like you think it was one of the immigrants."

"How the hell should I know? That's supposed to be your job. But I'll tell you," his eyes were red, and his face had grown to match them, "whoever did it is going to answer to me first. Anton was still one of us."

"'One of us.' And how long have you been working here?"

He held his nose up. "I got here ten months ago."

"Just after Anton did," Nigel guessed.

"I don't know, maybe. What does that matter?"

"You asked me to investigate. I'm just getting all the facts." Furrowing his brow, Nigel quickly glanced down at the list again. "Wait, how many snow hydrologists are there?"

"I'm the only one right now. Gregor went back t—"

Nigel waved his hand, "Yeah, yeah. Are you sure that knife was covered up before yesterday?"

"What are you talking about?"

"The snow, covering the knife I found. Didn't Catherine show you?"

"She didn't show me anything. What knife?"

Nigel slowly put his coffee cup down on the floor and a small custodial robot meandered over to pick it up. "She told me she talked to a precipitation guy about some snow. We found a knife over where the big man kicked the bucket. I had to dig it out. She said it was under too much snow to have fallen the day before."

"Well, there's some kind of mistake there, mate. She never talked to me about it. Maybe she looked at the readings we had, maybe there was just a ton of snow you pulled up and you didn't hear her properly."

"Ozzy found him around 4:30 a.m. How much snow could have fallen since 2:00 to 4 a.m. yesterday?"

"Well, the snow isn't really falling, it's being blown around during the storm. But the continent's increasing temperature and rising ocean levels are causing more actual precipitation and much more aggressive windstorms."

"Yeah, thanks professor. Just give me a number."

"I'm trying to tell you that it's not exact. But where we are, it increased about a meter. Three feet. How deep was the knife?"

"About three feet."

"You're sure?"

Nigel stood up to show him the picture. "I think we've got ourselves a nice little piece of evidence there, wouldn't you say?"

"It's a tad dodgy, yeah. Does it have a name or fingerprints or anything?"

"Don't you worry your big head about that Carl. Now, if you don't want your neck broken for a couple bucks, I suggest you direct me to the quartermaster."

"Fine." Carl walked rapidly out, not waiting for Nigel to catch up.

CHAPTER VIII

THE YEAR 2016

I came up to their house, but without a car in front, I was not sure anyone was even home. Overhead, thick clouds were accumulating as the afternoon transitioned to evening. I knocked on the door and Jordan answered, clearly not expecting company. Her hair was dark and matted, her nose was red, and she was in a faded pink bathrobe and slippers. Her glassy eyes rose to my face. "Inspector?"

"You can call me Nate. Sorry to disturb you. I just received some new information and wanted to just ask a few follow up questions if that is alright."

She cleared her throat and opened the door

wider. "I guess that's okay. Anything I can do to help."

"Is your husband home?"

"No, he's still at work." She led me inside. It was a breath of fresh air compared to the clutter and claustrophobia of Mrs. McKraney's residence. "You'll have to excuse me," she said, blowing her nose. "I seem to have a case of the sniffles. Probably from the plane." She sat on the couch, and I in the recliner. I took out my phone to record our conversation.

"That's right, your trip to Rio. How long were you there?"

"It was almost two weeks. Sorry, do you want some tea or anything?"

"No, no, I am okay. I don't want to take up too much of your time, seeing as how you are ill."

"Really, are you sure? It's no trouble. I already have a kettle on."

"Really, I am fine, thanks. Although, if it is not any trouble, I would like to see some of your vacation photos. My fiancée and I were thinking of going there on our honeymoon."

"Absolutely!" She took out her phone and scrolled through photos, describing in painful detail where each was taken and why it was significant.

I nodded along, photo after photo, finally asking, "Wow, look at that. Do you mind if I look closer?" when I saw a picture taken with both of them in the frame. She handed me the phone and I pretended to accidentally tap the top right corner, revealing the picture's timestamp in so doing. It really was taken the week before, making it unlikely that the couple personally delivered the recent packages.

I handed the phone back, suffering through more of the vacation album until I heard, "And this, yeah, I think this is the last one before we left. It's a beautiful—"

"Oh boy, look at that! May I?" I said, interrupting. She handed me the phone once more and I pulled the same maneuver, revealing the timestamp to be the day before Liza's break-in. *Which means they would not have been monitoring our conversation. At least, not over a live feed. Would they have arrived in time to watch two weeks of data?* Any theory of their guilt seemed to be slowly falling apart.

Again, I handed the phone back. "Well, I just

came to tell you that we think the break-in was perpetrated by a local prowler, a repeat offender who came from the woods behind your house. Mrs. McKraney said that she saw this person at 11:25 walking around in the trees. You were talking with Angelo at the time, correct?"

"Yes, that's right. Fernando checked the time twice."

"And nothing?"

"No, at least I didn't notice anyone. Sometimes kids walk through there though to have parties and stuff. But you can ask Fernando when he comes home if you want."

"I might, if it's not an imposition."

"Not at all, anything to help keep the neighborhood safe."

"There is another thing I need to ask. I would have preferred to ask both of you but…"

"Yes?" She blew her nose with a balled-up tissue.

"You told me you, or at least your husband did, that you did not know Hazel, your next-door neighbor very well, the woman who died last month. And yet, Mrs. McKraney made it seem like you and the late Ms. Berkley communicated quite often."

Jordan blew her nose furiously, squirming on the couch all the while. "No, she's mis, she's mistaken. We hardly saw her." Her gaze was buried in her tissue along with her snot.

I pressed a little harder. "And Liza said you went to the funeral, that you gave her a tiny interrogation of sorts when she first moved in."

"I—we..." She began to shake, then burst into tears, sobbing quietly. It made me both satisfied and immensely uncomfortable all at once.

"Tell me what it is. I can help, whatever it is. Just give me the truth"— I made a gesture of turning the phone off and putting it on the coffee table—"and it can stay just between us if it has to."

"You, you are working with the police?"

"Yes, but I have no reports to file. I report to no one. Not even Liza."

She seemed to take solace in my words, and calmed down a bit, still sniffling and blowing her nose. She picked at the edge of the pillow feverishly. "We didn't know what to do. And she was so..."

"You were friends with Hazel?" I asked, trying

to steer the discussion into a more chronologically comprehensible narrative.

"Yes. She was such a wonderful woman. She always was willing to help and to give, and she was one of my best friends. We miss her so much." A quiet sob.

"Naturally you do, of course. And what happened? Does it have to do with how she died?"

"I don't know. I think so. We didn't know if Liza, her granddaughter, if that's really her. We'd never met her in person. Do you know? Can you trust her?"

"Do I know... if Liza is her granddaughter? I am almost certain. Based on everything I have looked into so far. She is definitely the sole beneficiary."

Jordan loudly sniffed, rose, and drew her bathrobe about her in a sweeping motion. "I think I can trust you. I can trust you, can't I?"

"Of course. Here, if you want another look at my Private Investigator ID. I am working with the police on this case, I used to be a cop myself."

"Okay." She began walking out of the room. "Maybe this will help you in all this." She walked upstairs, there was some shuffling, and she came back down with a two-foot-long locked metal box, a foot deep. She sat down next to it on the couch. "She gave this to us. But you have to promise not to give it to Liza until you're sure, absolutely sure she is who she says she is."

"I promise I will. But Mrs. McKraney recognized her. Don't you trust her judgement?"

"I don't know. I don't know. Hazel made us, made me swear to protect what was in this box. It's her research, notes, and measurements and things. I never really knew what she was working on, she didn't like to talk about it. But a couple months before she passed, she came here and gave us this. Told us to keep the papers safe for her, she thought someone was after them. She thought she could trust us with them until she needed her notes again, and she wanted to keep them close by."

"I'll bet this is what the perp was looking for. Or something to do with this. Did she give you any other instructions?"

"Just that we should keep it hidden and that she would be back for it soon."

She hefted the box and I accepted it with both arms. I rose. "Thank you so much for your time and cooperation. Hopefully I will have some good news the next time I see you."

"Thank you. I hope so." She held a tissue to her nose. "Have a good night."

I started walking with the box and stopped. "Actually, do you mind if I leave this here for a minute? I want to pull my truck up in case anyone is watching."

"Of course."

"Oh, and I think Mrs. McKraney needs her casserole dish back." At that, Jordan's eyebrows raised.

I came back with the truck and parked it as far up the driveway as I could, diagonally, so that the passenger side was at an obscured viewpoint from the street. I smuggled the box into the Nate-mobile as best I could, then made tracks for my office.

CHAPTER IX

THE YEAR 2076

They arrived at the quartermaster's station, not too far from the lounge. Although, nothing seemed to be too far from anything, Nigel noticed. Carl stalked off without saying a word, leaving Nigel standing in front of a cage, behind which sat a burly man, not quite the size of Anton. *But big enough to break his neck.* His job was to dole out equipment and supplies, keeping track of the ever-fluctuating inventory. The lighting behind the man, sitting on his stool in front of his counter flickered almost imperceptibly. But it was enough to draw Nigel's attention to the stockpile of assorted supplies behind the quartermaster, including a box marked with a square cross. And that was when Nigel understood the need for a cage.

"What's up?" Nigel asked, speaking through the bars.

"Hey man, what you need, I ain't got all day." The man's deep, gravelly voice was offset by a Russian accent that was so thick and comical, Nigel thought he was talking to a cartoon supervillain. Now that Nigel could see him better, the quartermaster was large, but less of a mechanical-engineer-large, and more of a never-leaves-his-stool-for-extended-periods-large.

"You got drugs back there?" asked Nigel, nodding to the piles and shelves of boxes and the door that lay beyond them.

"Not for you, bud-dy. Now keep walking."

Nigel put his badge up against the bars of the cage. "Your man Anton was killed. I need some answers."

"What'd you want from me? He was on drugs?"

"Not that I know of. Just asking. Although he had a lot of vodka. He get that from you?"

"What this look like? Liquor store? He came in here, sure. For tools, harnesses, those type things.

He got vodka from village. Immigrant merchants. Don't blame me."

"Fine, fine. How about knives? I found a knife at the crime scene. Catherine said it came from here. Was it Anton's?" Nigel showed him a picture of it through the bars.

The man barely leaned forward to look at it. "I don't know. People lose stuff."

"Who was the last person to check out a knife?"

The quartermaster said nothing for a good minute, staring at Nigel, then he looked down at something on the counter. "Looks like Ivan was."

"When was that?"

"A week ago, Thursday."

Nigel wrote down *Ivan.* "That's not very helpful. You got anything else for me?"

"You need something from here?" the man asked pointed behind him.

"Do you have a magnifying glass?"

"I got microscope."

"No thanks." Nigel leaned on the bars. "Did you know Anton?"

"Everybody knew Anton. Now go. I got no information." The man tapped nervously on the counter, clearly intimidated by the detective.

Nigel pressed harder. "Why do you say that? That everybody knew him? Seems like there are a lot of people here, he's more of a behind the scenes kind of guy."

"He was always talking, like you. Always had something to say to everybody. Never shut up. And was always in gym. I caught him snooping around while they were closing this building."

"Why were you still here?"

"I am always last to leave. Everyone knows this. Go bother someone else with your questions."

"Alright pal, uh, what was your name again?"

The quartermaster hesitated. "Ivan. Ivan Egorov," he said gruffly.

"Lot of you Ivans around here. You're not terrible, are you?"

Ivan's scowl did not waver. "Very funny. Now, I have business to—"

"Watching movies?" interjected Nigel. Ivan's features betrayed his surprise and he sat in dumb silence, not able to come up with a quick response.

"Let me ask you something, Ivan." Nigel was leaning at a slant with his elbow on the counter in front of the bars. "Do you have a list with all these names of people who checked things out, or are you just working from memory?"

"I have list. What I tell you is accurate."

Nigel put on a sly smile in faux friendliness. "Do you mind if I have a look at that?"

Ivan the terrible quartermaster stood awkwardly up from his stool, and not without effort. "No, no. That is for quartermasters only."

"Why?"

"There are medical... purchases. Its private." Ivan began stumbling back, turning to go through the door to the back.

Nigel leaned both elbows on the counter, facing away from Ivan. He raised his voice enough to compensate for their increased vicinity. "Well, I guess I could get Catherine to request it from you, on my behalf that is. She might like to know what I find too."

Ivan stopped. He pulled up his pants over his belly, and slowly walked back to the counter. "Here," he said, handing Nigel a small screen dedicated to its one task of list making.

Nigel turned again, feinting surprise. "Why thank you, good sir! I will make sure your superiors know of your unwavering cooperation. Nigel scrolled through and found the most recent transaction. "Ah, I see Carl checked out a knife earlier this week. Slipped your mind?"

"Uh, yes, I forgot. But he doesn't need know where you learned this."

Nigel winked. "Of course, of course. Thanks for your time Ivan. I'll keep this list if you don't mind."

Ivan visibly grimaced.

Nigel roamed around more of the main building in search of Carl yet again. When Carl was nowhere to be found, he searched the other buildings as well. He found the gym where Anton supposedly worked out, but there was no locker or anything to suggest it.

He also found the employees' sleeping quarters, which were much nicer than the arrangements the residents had in the shelters outside, although they were still a tight fit. All the original researchers who still worked at the base stayed in the building's sleeping quarters, as well as other main staff. But they were packed together, practically on top each other in bunk beds, and any rooms were separated only by curtains. Nigel could envision Anton and his wife being offered these accommodations and refusing. That gave Nigel an inkling of where Carl might be.

But before he could leave, he received a message on his phone. *Detective Nigel. This is Dr. Jakobi. The fingerprinting you asked for is finished. I am in the sick bay.*

Walking back to the gym, Nigel asked a lady on a treadmill three times where the sick bay was. The first two times, she did not hear him. The third time, after turning off her music, it became apparent that she only spoke Russian, and instead of pressing the issue further, Nigel resolved to find it on his own. After going up a level and finding the dining room, he went back to the main research area on the ground floor. He made the decision to take a sharp right through a door left partially open, just before the corridor that adjoined the main room and the storage room. Unlike most of the facility, it was silent. He kept walking, sure he would find the med bay or sick lab or whatever soon, when suddenly, he came upon and recognized the two guards from before. They were standing in front of a hard metal door just like any of the others, except for one thing. Slipping into the shadows, Nigel took a picture of the scene.

Two guards, a locked door with no window, and four inconspicuous surveillance cameras above the door which did not escape Nigel's keen eye. *Cameras.*

It would probably not be a good idea to reveal his presence to them yet, he reasoned. He did his best impression of the ninja that killed Anton and made a silent retreat.

Finally, after more wandering, he asked someone who was slaving away at something that looked important, for directions. He was led into the same corridor through which he first went to come across the body. Inside the service corridor was a narrow passage and a narrower door, upon which was emblazoned the words *SICK BAY.*

It did not appear practically situated to Nigel. It seemed that if there were an emergency, someone would be going through a lot of twists and turns to reach it.

He went in. The door closed, sliding automatically with a *shunt.* Dr. Jakobi was the anomaly in an otherwise sterile environment filled with carefully organized medical equipment in labeled cabinets and drawers. An operating table of sorts dominated the room, and a row of empty beds lined the back wall.

"Helluva time finding the place, doc," Nigel said.

Dr. Jakobi sat in a shiny stool much nicer than Ivan's had been, flipping through some sort of paper binder, an act looked down upon in an age of less and less trees, now one of the world's most valuable resources. "Your fingerprints are over there on the table."

Nigel scooped up the machine he had given to Dr. Jakobi for the task. "Good job, doc. Are yours in here too?"

The doctor whirled on him, "Mine? Of course not."

Ever the diplomat, Nigel said, "Well, I need to separate yours from the rest after all. You did examine the body, didn't you?"

Dr. Jakobi grumbled something under his breath and swiped the fingerprinting machine from Nigel's grasp. He put the tip to his fingers, one at a time, then input his name when finished. As he was staring down at it, deciding whether or not to give it back, Nigel snatched it from his grasp. "Anyone give you trouble?" he asked.

"Everyone. Turns out people aren't too keen on being implicated in a crime."

"You sure got that done quick, didn't ya?"

"I have ways of making people come to me. As you may have noticed."

"Looks like I picked the right guy. You sure you got everybody's?"

Jakobi turned back to his papers. "I'm sure. Everybody who's here."

Nigel started to leave, then stopped. "Hey, you ever treat a guy, probably over a hundred years old? Name's Alexi."

"Yes. He's 104. He has aches and pains, but he's used to the cold. A harmless old man."

Nigel nodded and walked out.

CHAPTER X

THE YEAR 2016

I walked into my office. Sam was at his desk reading a cheap detective novel and stuffing a Philly cheesesteak down his gullet. "Sam."

"Nate, I didn't know you were coming back. I'm getting ready to head out soon."

"Any more of that for me?" I asked, pointing toward the sub.

"Uh, I um, did you want—"

I said, "I'm joking," producing my plate of leftovers. "I had some really superb lasagna." I handed it to him, and he leaned back to put it in the mini fridge. "Bring your sandwich in the back. I want to discuss something with you."

We walked back into my office. Sam closed the

door behind us and sat in front of my desk, continuing to eat his greasy sandwich. With a clunk, I sat the box down on my desk. "You are pretty much caught up on this case so far, right?"

"I think so."

"Great. So, I have some new information about the cameras. Some of them were short-range, meaning our stalker had to be nearby."

"Well, we already knew that."

"Nearby as in, one of the neighbors had to have done it."

"Oh." He said, lowering the sandwich-half to his lap.

"I am almost positive that the couple next door was telling the truth, and they have an alibi. Plus, they give the neighbor across the street a good alibi too."

"Hm, okay."

"So, we are left with Old Mrs. McKraney (a small elderly woman with a cane) or the mother with two daughters, whom I have not visited. I will go see them first thing tomorrow. But the trouble is, we are still operating under the assumption that a man is our criminal, because of Liza's kitchen encounter and the size of those boot prints."

"Unless our guy is hiding in that house for sale."

"Yes, but it seems impractical. Not ruling it out though. I checked out the grandmother's old work, and it looks like the place was just recently cleared out. They completely closed up shop."

"A little suspicious." Sam went back to eating his sandwich.

"Oh, it gets better. After visiting the McKraney residence, I went back to visit Jordan and Fernando who gave me this:" I laid my hand on the box with a thud. "Apparently, Liza's grandma wanted her research notes on a project or something to be hidden." I opened my desk drawer and took out a lockpick set, making quick work of the box's small latch, which opened, clanging.

"Are they from her job or something else?"

"I really don't know, but I would be willing to bet they came from something she was doing at her job." I pulled several notebooks and loose papers from the box. Two USB's and a portable hard drive were at the bottom. "Jeez, none of this is even written in English."

"Let me see," said Sam, throwing out his sandwich wrappings.

"No, I mean literally. None of this has any words from the English language. I will need an expert to look at these." I locked everything back up in the box the way I pulled it out.

"So basically, someone was after the grandmother's research and it's probably one of the neighbors, only two of whom are men."

"That about wraps it up."

"So, you only have two potential suspects."

"Really only one. I feel like Liza would have seen Fernando's bushy moustache, even for a second. Besides, he was with his wife in Rio when those packages were delivered. And unless Angelo was working with someone else, he's off the hook too."

"Maybe he was distracting his neighbors while someone else broke into the house."

"It's possible, but riskier. A stranger would be easier to spot snooping around the neighborhood. And why would he want them out in the street facing her house while that was happening? This partner would have been a return customer too. I found his footprints at the house and the empty house directly across the street. To be fair though, that is the best theory we have."

Sam yawned. "What time is it? I should be headed home."

Then, it dawned on me. Muttering to myself, I began. "Unless... Wait! Sam! I think I know... maybe their alibi was not so airtight after all!"

"What do you mean?"

"The gold watch. Fernando had an obvious tan line under his designer watch." I began dialing the number I had written in my notebook. "Hi Jordan, Nate again. Yes, the detective. Is Fernando home yet? You did, oh well let me talk to him. Hi Fernando. Yes, I have it right here. I am not planning to do anything yet. I am just keeping it safe for now. Yes, that is correct. But just, yeah. Okay, I have something else I need to ask you though. When you came back from Rio, did you remember to set your watch back? Yeah, yes. You forgot about it until this morning. Right, and that would have been two hours ahead, correct? Okay, thank you. I promise I will. To the best of my ability. Thanks, bye. Yeah, you too, bye."

I hung up the phone. Sam asked, "What was that?"

"I am glad you asked Sam old chum! They were not talking to Angelo when they said they were.

Or more precisely, when they thought they were. What Fernando thought was 11:00 a.m. because he forgot to reset the time-zone shift on his watch, was actually only 9:00 a.m." I paced around the room, my footsteps growing more rapid. "And he said that Angelo was getting ready to leave around 1 p.m. But that would actually have been at 11 a.m., right as Mygan was leaving."

"Angelo's not looking so innocent anymore. What do you know about him?"

"Not much. He was not exactly cooperative when we went to talk to him. I know he has been there since before the couple moved in. I should take another look at the property records, see if I can dig a little deeper. You can go home if you want, I think I might be here a while."

"Glad I could help," Sam said, getting up. "Have a good night."

"Yeah, you too Sam."

I began my search hopeful. But the first thing I needed was the guy's last name. "That is, strange," I said, forgetting for a moment that Sam had left. The property's sale history did not list an Angelo. I texted Liza. *Hey, can you ask Mrs. M what Angelo's last name is? I might have a lead.*

A minute later she replied. *No prob.* And a few seconds after that, *She said she thinks its Melnyk.*

It's 'it's.'

What?

Sorry, never mind. Thanks for your help. Talk soon.

I spent the better part of an hour scouring the internet for a Floridian named Angelo Melnyk to no avail. At that point, I was sweating to a horrendous degree, and got up to steal the fan from Sam's office. I came back, rubbed my ironically dry eyes, and went back to the house's property record, convinced that "Angelo" was an assumed name. The record listed the house's owner as a Mr. Rurik Kuznetsov who made the purchase a year and a half before. *Rurik, where have I heard that name? Russian?* My fingertips began to tingle with excitement as I took out my phone and went through some of the photos that I had taken in the McKraney attic. And there it was. The name was on the back of a photograph which depicted a 20-year-old Rurik standing next to the late Mr. McKraney in 1992. With context I could place his face, and knew it was the same man.

The pieces were all falling into place. Rurik

came to the United States in 1991 on a work visa, before Truskol had opened its Florida office. According to Truskol's employee logs, Rurik was still working with the company. I was hard pressed to find much more information about the man, other than that he made a generous salary for business "consulting" and generally kept his head down. Also, he had earned his US citizenship after a year in the states, and in 2005, he was given a speeding ticket in Nebraska which he did not contest.

At this point, I was positive I had my man, not just for the packages and the break-in, but for Hazel's death as well. But without evidence, Johnson would not be granted a warrant to search his place for the recording setup, model plane, or anything else he may have stolen. I considered going to speak with him again but did not think tipping off such a careful man who could flee the country was such a good idea. Especially if a multibillion-dollar company like Truskol was behind him.

It was already getting late. I could have worked the rest of the night trying to dig up more information, but Truskol and Rurik both seemed good at covering their tracks. I called Truskol's main American office located in Boston, but a machine told me to call back the next day during work hours.

Finally, I packed up my gear, grabbed my cold lasagna, and locked up the office, deciding to stake-out Rurik's house until I could come up with a better plan of action. The sun was beginning to set, and I was glad for it. I drove home and retrieved the stakeout car, forsaking the more easily recognized Nate-mobile. I then drove to Liza's neighborhood, parking my car on the side of the road, way before the bend into the neighborhood's dead-end road. I was on the side closest to the empty house, directly behind it and up the street a ways. I had a direct line of sight to the house's backyard and could also see Rurik's backyard and the back half of his car sitting out front. That way, I could see if he left out the back, and I could see if he began driving and could follow him if he did. If he started walking out the front door however, I probably would not be able to see.

The light was on in the back room at the top floor. A couple of hours passed, and the night turned dark. I sipped some coffee, but not too much, so I would not have to pee. Not much happened, and no cars came or went. Knowing it was trash day, my plan was to wait for him to take out the trash so I could have a look inside the cans, maybe pull some prints. But as the hours stretched on, it seemed that would not be happening. He went down into the basement for a while, eventually seeming to go to bed, turning off all the lights. A quiet rumbling in my stomach grew more persistent, and I reached for the plate of leftover lasagna and greens to finish it off, all the while, keeping my eyes trained on Rurik's backdoor.

It looked like he would be going nowhere soon. Luckily, holding that lasagna in my hands gave me an idea. But it would be a two-man job. It was 4:30 a.m., and I drove home to get some rest.

The next morning, I called upon Mrs. McKraney. I tried to be discreet, parking at Liza's place and walking behind the houses, toward the end of the street. On the way there I noticed that Rurik's car was gone, and he appeared not to be home.

I eventually made my way to the McKraney porch and knocked on the door. "Well, well. Good morning young sir. I was just about to take Polly for her walk. She had a fitful night of sleep for some reason and got up three times. But do you know what? She got up right at the same time she always does for her walk. Tell me mister detective, how do dogs do it? I myself am quite exhausted from her shenanigans. Without my morning green tea, I don't know what I'd do. Anyway, Liza already left for a meeting I don't know when she'll be back. I didn't think *you* were coming back, running off the way you did, without so much as a bite of my tea cakes."

"Sorry about that, it was a time-sensitive issue. I actually did not come for Liza; I came here today to ask a big favor of you."

"Oh?"

"How long does it usually take Ru—Angelo to return your casserole dishes?"

"Angelo always returns them right away. I guess he eats them immediately, then puts the rest away for later. He's always home and he comes over right away. But he asked me not to make any more for him. Said he had a weak stomach or some such nonsense. I think he just feels uncomfortable with unrequited gifts. But I know he's fibbing because he always returns the dishes right away, so he must be eating them, no matter how many times he tells me he doesn't need anymore. He doesn't have anyone cooking for him you know, so I feel responsible."

Maybe he returns them so you will not drop in unexpectedly. "That is good to hear. If I can beseech you to please make a lasagna and deliver it to him, I can pay you for it and bring any supplies you need."

"Nonsense! I'd be happy to do it. He's a good man. I should have everything I need here. Did he send you here to ask me? That rascal!"

"Actually, it is for my investigation. I might also need to borrow the dish for a while if that is okay."

"I see. Well, anything to help with your investigation. I hope you know what you are doing young man."

"I believe I do. And Angelo has been here for closer to two years now, correct? I assume you baked him a lasagna when he first moved in?"

"Yes, why do you ask?"

"I just wanted to make sure I am on the right track. And when was the last time you talked to him?"

"Well, that was just yesterday when I went to tell him about that horrible break-in. He said you had questioned him about it, and he gave you all the information he had. That it was his duty to co-operate with the police, for the good of the neighborhood. He asked me in great detail whether I had seen or heard anything, and I told him what I told you. What a good neighbor and a conscientious citizen. Not like the kids these days."

I may have smirked. "Well anyway, thanks for your help. I have to run some errands and then I will be back. What time do you think you will have it ready to give him?"

"It should not take too long. I can get started right after Polly's walk. Maybe an hour and a half after that."

"Okay. And when you answer the door, make sure you are wearing oven mitts or something, just try not to grab the tray directly. Again, thanks so much for your assistance. You have been more helpful than you realize."

I went back to sit in my truck, then texted Johnson. *Think I have my guy. Are prints enough for a warrant?* After receiving no immediate reply, I gave the local university a call and was connected to a professor of nuclear physics.

"Hello. This is Professor Rubenstein." The professor's voice sounded dry and nasal.

"Hi, my name is Nathan Berkley. I thought you might be able to help me. I have some old notes of my grandmother's from before she passed. She was a physicist and engineer, and I was wondering if you could help me decipher them. I just want to know if they are worth keeping or if I should throw them out. She kept quite a lot of them."

"That sounds intriguing. I should be in my office after six, but you could just email me some examples of her work and that way I can give you your answer sooner."

"No, if it is alright, I would prefer to come in person. "

"Fine, fine. And what was your name again?"

"Nate."

"Okay then Mr. Nate, come by any time after six. I am also here tomorrow morning, but only before noon."

"Thanks, see you soon. Bye."

I hung up and dialed the number of Truskol headquarters. They put me on hold three times until I was finally transferred to a representative who only wasted my time, feeding me a line about the Florida office's closure being "due to budget issues" and that they expected the other American offices to remain open. The representative repeated the same thing four different ways without giving any more detail or information, finally putting me on hold again, then hanging up on me.

After two hours passed, I gave up, and returned my attention to lasagna. Out of the Nate-mobile's rear window, I saw that Rurik had returned home at some point, which I missed while I was on the phone. I also missed a text from Johnson. *Should be. Who's the guy?*

Grumpy neighbor. When can I hand them off?
Here till 3.

I got out and went back over to the McKraney residence. Her dog was on the porch half asleep and Mrs. McKraney was waiting for me just inside, her front door still open.

"Has the package been delivered?" I asked.

"Yes, yes, he received my lasagna. I gave it to him as he was getting out of his car. Didn't tell me where he had been, now that I think about it."

"I am guessing he still has to return the dish?"

"How fast do you think I am? I just got back."

"Hm. Do you mind if I wait here? I would like to take another look up in the attic."

"Oh, this again. Well I suppose that'd be fine,

just don't interrupt my show. It's coming on in a few minutes and I tolerate no interruptions. I can't properly start my day without my television programming. You're welcome to watch though. As long as you don't interrupt with questions, that is. My eldest son, when he was young, he would always interrupt, always, every time I tried to watch my shows. I had to start leaving him out in the yard."

"Ohhh...kay. Well, I will go upstairs. Thanks though."

Up in the musty dusty attic, I found the light switch and worked my way over to the boxes, where I had searched the day before. I rifled through, looking higher and lower, hither and thither, but was unable to find any other pictures or references to Rurik. So, I rededicated my efforts to looking for more of George and Hazel's shared work. Although much of it was grouped together, an easy task, it was not. Especially since I had very little idea what I was even looking at.

By the time I had managed to contain it all within a few manila envelopes, I heard voices downstairs. At first, I thought it could be Liza, but one of them sounded vaguely like a man's voice.

I fought the urge to go down, as the best course of action was undoubtably to stay hidden where I was. The voices quieted and, after a tick, Mrs. McKraney called for me at the bottom of the attic ladder. I went down, holding my breath after upsetting a particularly thick mote cloud.

"He brought it back just like I said he would. Always a gentleman."

"Yes, thank you Mrs. McKraney. And you used oven mitts?"

"I did, I had them next to me on the couch. But why you did all this is beyond me. Anyway, I left it over on the kitchen counter if you want it."

"Thanks." I walked over with my little black briefcase full of fingerprinting tools that I had carried with me from the truck. "You can watch if you want. What I need to do is lift Rurik's fingerprints off this glass. We can—"

"Rurik?"

"Oh, sorry. I might as well tell you. Angelo is not his birth name."

"Really? You shouldn't go digging around in people's personal information like that. It's unconstitutional. His name is his business. Personal business. Just because he changed his name, he is suddenly a suspected criminal? I tell you, if it's a man you're looking for, there's already one right next door. He even has a suspicious-looking moustache."

"Well, if he is innocent this will quickly clear his name, and I can move on to other suspects."

Her show came back on and Mrs. McKraney moved back to the couch with a swiftness of which I did not think her capable. I took my time and was able to pull two full handprints off the bottom of the container. When I was finished with the tray, I wrapped it in plastic to take with me just in case. I packed up and went over to the door, opening my mouth to bid my farewell, then decided against it and left quietly.

CHAPTER XI

THE YEAR 2076

In the list Oslow had given him, Nigel found Carl's name among the residents. For a reason Nigel could not yet prove, Carl decided to live outside the research facility, just like Anton and some of the other workers.

With his chauffeur Oslow busy, Nigel took it upon himself to commandeer a snowmobile. Outside, the onslaught of snowy madness had subsided, and the fresh white landscape had a dignity to it, one of serene calmness.

Navigating the grid of tiny abodes, Nigel found the number denoting Carl's unit, not far from Anton and Alexi's. Nigel had a look around. A little electric griddle sat by the door, protected by an impressive fortress made of packed snow. A teeny flag jutted from the outer wall of the fortress. Nigel knocked. There was no answer. He tried the handle. It was locked. He could hear noises coming from inside, so he waited. He waited, then waited some more. Finally, someone opened the door, to see who had been knocking, probably expecting that person to have already left.

"Hello again, Carl," Nigel said, unmoved from his knocking spot. Carl's eyes were bloodshot.

"What now?"

"I have a list here. Says you checked a knife out of supplies not too long ago. Any comment?"

"What of it? I lent mine to someone. I wanted a new one."

"Who?"

"Doesn't bloody matter, it's not the one you're looking for, it was days ago. Now sod off." With that Carl slammed the door, successfully ending the conversation. Nigel kicked a hole in the snow fortress wall which came tumbling down.

The next name on Nigel's list of questionees was Catherine's.

On his way back, Nigel received a voice message from Janice at the UN. "Sending the plane back,

Nige. Call me when it comes in. There were some interesting results."

He called Catherine and asked her to meet him out front. After a surprisingly brief wait, she met him outside.

"Any news detective?"

"I've learned a few things. Best not to spread rumors though. But your man Carl told me that you never spoke to him about the knife. He said it very well could have been dropped by the murderer. That we had plenty of snow come down."

Catherine shifted her weight uncomfortably. "No, he told me it was too deep. Maybe I misunderstood. What difference is it? Not much difference it can be, can it?"

"Maybe, maybe not. With how hard the ice was underneath; it would've been hard to shove down. But now I know it could have been dropped, which seems the more likely scenario."

"I see."

"By the way, that list you gave me. It says you have one hundred and sixteen employees, but only a hundred and eight are listed."

"You counted them?"

"I did. And the doc only gave me a hundred and eight sets of prints."

"It must be mistake, then. We have people come and then they go. It will be fixed. Right away."

Before he could respond, Nigel received a notification that his plane was coming in and would land in about ten minutes. When Nigel looked up from the message he had just received, Catherine was already retreating into the building. He was about to pursue the issue, but decided to go wait for the plane, which would land where it had before, and no closer for whatever reason.

He made his way to the flattened sheet of ice where he first touched down and waited for what felt like much more than ten minutes. His coat's heater, while an invaluable asset, failed to keep his toes warm. When the plane silently set down, Nigel clambered aboard as quickly as any human has ever clambered aboard anything.

Now aboard the empty plane, he tried to get ahold of Janice, but there was no response. He sat and considered the case so far, deciding to instead give Anton's wife a try. Her contact information was included in the casefile.

"Hello?" asked a jaded and trepidatious voice in perfect English.

"Hi ma'am, this is detective Nigel Woods with the UN inspection office. Is this Mrs. Nina Minsky?"

"Yes, this is she."

"I'm calling about your husband."

"Obviously."

"I have a couple questions for you. Um, when was the last time you saw Anton?"

There was a pause so long, it was probably in its third trimester. "A while. Around two months."

"You weren't getting along?" Nigel guessed.

She sighed. "We loved each other. But there were... irreconcilable differences. Anton wanted me to stay, but I needed a break. Especially from that dreary place."

"And where are you now?"

"Iceland. For the foreseeable future."

"Look, if you have any information that can help, now's the time."

"I can't help you; I've been gone for months. Maybe you should ask his buddy Carl." She abruptly disconnected the call.

Nigel closed his mouth, not able to bring the

next part of the conversation into existence. He called back three times to no avail. *What is it with people hanging up on me?*

Taking Mrs. Minsky's advice, Nigel hopped on the internet to do a little digging into Carl's past. Carl had no arrest record, a terrible credit score, and a master's degree in Water Science Policy and Management from Oxford University. He had moved to Russia only a few months after Anton.

As Nigel tried desperately to recall an important scrap of information at the back of his mind, the cabin's main monitor started blinking. *INCOMING CALL.* "Answer call," he said, and Janice's face came up on the display.

"Nige!"

"Jan!"

"You want the good news or the bad news?" she asked.

"Just get to it. I got pasta waitin' for me back home."

Janice leaned out of frame for a few seconds, looking through something. "The knife got a hit. The prints. They came up in the general criminal database. They belong to a Rurik Kuznetsov. Manslaughter, burglary, theft, bunch of other stuff. But that was all info from our UN system. I can't find his actual file anywhere."

"Hold that thought." Nigel produced his phone and started searching through the list of employees, then the list of residents. "I can't find a 'Rurik' anywhere here. Maybe he was one of the missing workers."

"The what?"

"Nothing. What else you got?"

"There was a little chip in the blade, snagged some fibers. Looks like they were nylon fibers. They could've come from a lot of stuff, but nothing easy to cut through. Moving on." The camera panned over to a corpse lying on a table in the middle of the room in an undignified manner. It was Anton. "It's hard to tell exactly how his neck broke," Janice said. "But something with a whole lot of force was responsible. It also looks like he was hit over the head"—she ran a gloved hand over the area in question—"but not hard enough to do real damage. It might have knocked him out at the most. No drugs or anything in his system. Last meal was potatoes and peas. That's about all I got. Oh, and his hands are a little scratched up. Could be any reason for that. The scratches don't look recent or defensive."

"Any alcohol in his system?"

"Nope. Not as far as I could tell."

"Thanks for the quick turnaround on this one."

"Whoa, did Nigel Woods just say, 'thank you?!'" She swooned. "I must really be somebody special."

"Don't make me take it back. Wait, what was the bad news?"

"I don't know. I just thought saying that would make my good news sound better."

Nigel grunted. "Goodbye," he said, jamming a finger downward, turning off the screen.

Nigel began to fiddle with the fingerprint machine he had taken back from doctor Jakobi. He connected the fingerprint information for the employees and fingerprints from the crime scene in order to compare them with those found on the knife. The fingerprinting software to which they were connected, cross-referenced the different sets and found no matches with any of the employees, or even Anton himself, who had in fact been trying to get in the building, based on the handprints he had left by the door. This made Nigel think that perhaps he had been running from his attacker. But who could scare such an enormous man, even with a knife?

Nigel went to the back of the cabin, using the plane's computer to gain direct access to UN records. Which were all records. He typed in the name Rurik Kuznetsov, expecting a police file, a passport, or birth certificate. But all that was presented was an arrest record with his photo and prints, and a few local news reports from the American East Coast. The reports detailed the activities of a man who had broken into his neighbor's home and spied on her for months. He was arrested, but never served the time after sentencing, fleeing the country while still on probation. He had been an employee at Truskol Energy Corp. which Nigel also looked up and found to be a now dissolved organization. Nigel vaguely remembered hearing about its troubles concerning the international legality of some of the company's practices.

The news reports focused on the amount of effort that went into Rurik's crimes, as well as the man who helped solve the case, a private detective named Nathan Gallup who was basically a local superhero. Interested, Nigel dug into the PI's past and found a dozen or so similar instances where the man was featured in news stories helping the police bring criminals to justice during his exceptionally illustrious career.

But Nigel needed to find out who Rurik was and how he came to be in Antarctica. There were no longer police in the southern United States, and most of the people involved in the case were dead. He sent a request to his office's research department in the hopes of finding the original files, which were apparently lost, either intentionally or otherwise. He might have an easier time, he decided, working backwards, trying to find out how Rurik made it to Antarctica, and whether he had first fled to Russia.

Once again, Nigel made a phone call. This time, to his UN buddy, Frank, who operated inside the Russian government and owed him a favor. After a short call, Frank (not being a detective) agreed to help Nigel under the condition that Nigel let him fly in the jet on his next assignment, a bargain to which Nigel agreed.

He hung up and told the computer to blast some rock music while he considered his options.

At the moment, Nigel had little to go on concerning this new suspect, and tracking Rurik, who could be any age and operating under any kind of alias, felt daunting. In Nigel's favor, however, was the fact that the storm would have prevented a lone escape to any neighboring colonies, the nearest being over twenty miles away. While Frank trawled for information, Nathan the PI would be Nigel's best bet for digging up more information on sneaky old Rurik.

Connecting to the main internet, Nigel went online and found the business of detective Nathan Gallup, still operating, but in Maine instead of in Florida as it once had. The business's website looked old and unmanaged, but it gave him the information he needed. Nigel wanted to just call but knew from experience that people wasted less of his time if he simply showed up in person to get the information he needed. This oftentimes cut out any middleman as well. With a jet plane whose solar cells were fully fueled, it would be no time at all, and he could be back in Antarctica within a few short hours. *Oh boy!* The ridiculousness of using sarcasm in his own head was not lost on Nigel.

He sent a message to Catherine and Oslow,

telling them to make sure no one left the colony while he was gone, then bade his automatic pilot to take flight, heading for Portland, Maine.

CHAPTER XII

THE YEAR 2016

I drove to the station, letting Johnson know beforehand that I had the lasagna prints and was only looking for a direct match. It was good to have a point-person in the department, otherwise, things usually took twice as long. Either that, or I was stonewalled by people in the department who considered my cases of a less urgent nature.

I pulled up to the police station. Johnson was near the entrance talking to a kid in a purple hoodie who ran off. I got out, holding my little black briefcase.

"Can't park there. 'Fraid I'll have to give you a ticket." Johnson said smugly as I approached.

"Good morning to you too."

"Not mornin' anymore."

"Whatever. Thanks for coming out, you probably saved me from another run-in with Henry."

"I've a duty to serve. So, you think you got yer guy?"

"Well, he is using a fake name, has all his windows covered, is a bit of an asshole, and—get this—he worked at the same company with Hazel. He is the stalker. She was trying to hide some papers from somebody, and I think that is what he was after, not the granddaughter. Maybe he thought Liza knew where they were, I don't know. But if we can place him in that bathroom, maybe we can find some real evidence and start asking the tough questions. If we get lucky, he might spill on his boss or maybe an accomplice, although everything points to his acting alone."

"You talk to him yet?"

"No, he should not be tipped off, unless one of the neighbors says something to him." I handed Johnson the prints. "How long will these take to run?"

"I don't know, we're backed up with murders right now. It's a simple match... I could probably have it by end of day if I annoy 'em enough."

"Thanks, I really appreciate it."

"And then what? You want me to get a warrant for, what are we looking for?"

"The surveillance setup. I figure, if he already knows we have his cameras, we might be running out of time before he destroys it all or throws everything out."

"Uh huh. Well, I can try. You're on the case, but I'm warning you now, I might have to bring him in as a suspect and take his prints directly to get the warrant. I'll explain the situation though."

I shook his hand and started walking back to the truck. "Thanks again," I said, rubbing my hand to try and alleviate its newfound soreness.

He said, "I'll call," and went back inside.

I checked the time and drove to my office to collect the metal box for my appointment with the professor. I was in high spirits, as everything had been moving swiftly, and I hoped it would continue that way. If I were lucky, I could wrap the whole case within a week, a rare delight.

I parked in front of my office, and as I approached my building, I spotted the main entrance with its door slightly ajar. I began formulating the words I would need to chastise Sam, but then remembered he had the day off. The only other person who would have left it open would be the landlord, but he usually called before coming by.

Cautiously, I stepped closer and could hear the burglar alarm going off. *Ohhh shit.* I reached toward the security panel to turn it off. Part of the panel was hanging off, as if someone had tried to pry it open. I punched in the code with my shirt-sleeve, so as not obscure any fingerprints left by the person whom I assumed to be a criminal. From what I could tell, the person visited the office, saw no one was home, forced his/her way in, the alarm went off, he/she tried to turn it off but was unsuccessful, rifled through a couple drawers, was still spooked by the alarm, and ran off.

And then I facepalmed. Rurik had been gone when I was at the house. He must have left just as I arrived at Liza's, and I had not seen him leave. *Maybe he saw me carry the box into my truck yesterday. What does he think it is?*

In case I was still being watched (he had a track record) I did not immediately run into my office for the box Jordan had given me. Instead, I calmly walked into my room, shut the door, and began inspecting everything from top to bottom. I started by checking the Wi-Fi to make sure no new devices were connected. I looked for any new objects, then checked the power outlets to make sure nothing was plugged in. Finally, I turned off all the lights and covered the window with a rug after shuttering its blinds. I shined a flashlight slowly around the room, then an infrared light, but nothing visibly reflected back at me. Confident in the quality of my search for hidden cameras, I let light back in and cleaned up a little, closing the drawers that were left open.

I then had a choice to make. I could either call to report the break-in or make it in time for my appointment with the university professor. Choosing the latter, I called Sam and let him know what had happened and that he should be careful, to also be sure to lock the door to his house. Then I asked him pleadingly to come to work, imploring him to deal with the police, taking prints from the security panel if he could. After a roundabout sort of discussion, he reluctantly agreed.

After persuading Sam, I climbed up on my desk and popped out the ceiling panel, dropping dirt and dust directly into my eyes. My hand blindly groped around in the ceiling's recesses before land-ing on the metal box. I pulled it slowly and carefully from the ceiling, shutting my eyes all the while, and retrieved it without further damage to my vision or patience. I then bundled it in a jacket and left for the college.

————————————

I arrived on campus, but quickly lost my way. After asking several people for directions, I finally found Professor Rubenstein's office down a shiny hallway and knocked.

"Come in" said an irritated voice. I came in. "Are you one of mine?" asked the tiny bespectacled man, seemingly perched atop stacks of papers.

"Um, no. My name is Nate, we spoke on the phone."

"Oh, oh yes, please have a seat. I'm afraid I don't have much time. You just need me to identify some, what? Research notes? Theses? Unpublished science papers?"

I moved some notebooks off the lone chair so I could sit. "Sorry, I am not really sure. She did say she wanted them kept safe."

"Well, let's see if there's anything worth publishing." I handed him the entire box and he began to sift through. He started by glancing at the loose papers, then looked through the notebooks and folders. He did not spend much time on any one page before moving to the next, and he did it all in complete silence. A few times, his eyebrows came together, and he frowned hard, but still he remained silent. This went on for some time until, still frowning, he finally said, "Do you have anything else?"

"There should be some flash drives and a hard drive at the bottom."

He pulled them out, replacing some of the paperwork. With his hand supporting his chin, he sat in front of his computer monitor, unmoving, constantly scrolling his mouse and frowning. "The hard drive and the USB are encrypted," he said at last.

"What about the other USB?" I asked.

"It has a few pictures of machine components of some kind. And the rest"—he picked up a pile of papers and let them fall back to the desk—"are, well, I can't help you. There are some comprehensible formulas, but everything is obscured by some sort of cypher. No one can understand this without a decoder or a key. These diagrams look like they might be for some kind of container for a nuclear reaction, but really, I'm not sure. It's not based on anything I've ever seen. And based on the way the parts are broken up, it looks like that was done intentionally. I'm sorry but I just can't help you."

It took me a few seconds to absorb everything. This lady was careful. "Fascinating. Grammy always did love her puzzles. Well, I do have one more thing." I produced a folder with some of George's paperwork. "These were some of the notes her partner had. They worked on at least one project together."

"Ah," said the professor. These are much clearer. However, these papers near the bottom also start using the code. It looks like they used the same cipher. If you can get your hands on the cipher key, maybe I can help you. But until then," he handed me back the papers and the box, "these are useless."

I shook his hand and thanked him for his time, making my way through the campus maze, paying attention to the people around me in case I was being followed.

As I navigated my way back, I called Sam. "Hey, any news?"

"The boys in blue just left. I'll be joining them soon."

"Get the prints?"

"Yeah, it took a good bit of arguing. I tried to explain the situation, and I had the kit ready, so they finally agreed to take them. But yeah, they're on record now."

"You are a saint, Sam."

"Yeah, yeah. Goodbye."

Back in my truck, I was on the road again, driving to put the box away and wait for the fingerprint results Johnson owed me. I thought long and hard about a safer location for the box but could come up with nothing better than the ceiling in my office. On the way, Johnson called.

"Go for Nate."

"It's a match."

I almost swerved out of my lane while emphatically pumping my fist in the air. "Great news. Also... someone broke into my office. I think it was the same guy, but I am not sure." Johnson sighed as I continued. "I might have a couple partial prints there, your guys have them on file. We can circle back to that. So, warrant?"

"I'm on my way to try and get it. I'll let ya

know. I'm just asking for the recordings, right? Anything else you think is in there?"

"No, but I am sure we will find some other items of interest."

"Okay, I'll let ya know. Bye."

"Bye."

Back at my office, I replaced the box and cleaned up the rest of the mess that our intruder left behind. Then, I called poor Liza. "Hi Liza. I have news."

"What kind of news?" she asked tiredly.

"It is, uh, I think it is good news. But first, did Angelo, the neighbor guy across the street, did he ever come over to your place? Maybe to use the bathroom?"

"No, he hasn't spoken to me since I got here. Oh god, why?"

"Well, we found his prints in your bathroom, and the evidence I found so far points to his being the person who broke in. Now, it is not for sure, but we are working on getting a warrant to search his home. What do you know about him? Do you know him well?"

"No, not really. He moved in about two years

ago, maybe less. That's all I really know. Grandma never talked about him."

"That's okay. We should have the information we need. Hopefully that warrant comes through soon. Until then, I can keep an eye on him, make sure he does not do anything sneaky. Sneaky-er."

"Thanks, so much Nate. You've done an amazing job. I'll have to buy you dinner after all this."

"Oh, well I never say no to free food."

She chuckled. "I've noticed. Well, hey I've got to go. But thank you again, really."

"No problem." I hung up and went over to the mini fridge to steal any food Sam had left behind. I took my gear, my car, and half a tuna melt, back to my spot behind Rurik's house and waited. And waited. I put my windows down, but when night-time came, the noise its creatures brought with it grew deafening.

Around midnight, Rurik left his house, clad in black, and snuck out his back door. I sunk low in my seat, but he seemed not to spot me. He took a wide, circuitous route across the street to Liza's house, avoiding detection. Or so he thought. I had my finger on my camera button and pressed it generously all the while. I could barely see what he was doing, but decided not to leave the car, to avoid tipping him off. It looked like he was peering through the windows, of the house with a flashlight. As I took out my phone to call the police, Fernando exited his house, spooking Rurik, who ran back into the shadows and around to the other side of the house. Luckily, this gave me a perfect angle from which to snap a picture of Rurik's face with my infrared lens. Fernando was having a smoke, and Rurik decided not to take his chances, retreating backward along the path he had taken from his house.

I spent a few more hours waiting for him to resurface, but the cold coffee I had left over from the day before was not enough to forestall the sandman, and I quite unprofessionally fell into slumber. The next morning, I was awoken by the ringing of my phone. I squinted hard against the all-consuming light of day, fighting a losing battle. "Hello?" I asked.

"No, 'Gopher Nate?'" asked Johnson.

"Gopher? Oh god!"

"What? What happened?"

"My neck! I think I slept on it wrong."

"Jeezus, did you just wake up?"

"Ugh. Do you have good news for me?"

"I do. We got the warrant. We'll be there in an hour. You coming?"

With one hand caressing the back of my tender neck, I raised the other one which was holding the phone, in order to sniff my armpit. "I am already here."

"Even better. Oh, I checked the prints from your office alarm."

"And?"

"They're a match. Even if we don't find anythin' today, we're still bringin' this guy in."

"Awesome," I said, blinking, desperately trying to regain some semblance of normal vision. "You're not bringing SWAT or anything, are you?"

Johnson laughed.

————————————————

An hour later, two cop cars pulled up to Rurik's house, sirens off. I met Johnson on the lawn. "Thanks a lot Phil. You have been a real pal."

"And don't ya forget it."

There were four officers in total, and as Johnson, his female partner (whose name I could never remember), and I, went up to knock on the door, the other two officers went around back. Johnson did his police pound a few times. We waited, then heard shouting coming from the backyard. Johnson drew his gun and we made our way around. Sure enough, Rurik had tried to make his escape, and was now on the ground in cuffs. He looked grumpy. But then again, that seemed to be his default expression.

I oversaw the officers as they went in and did a detailed search of the premises, while one of them babysat an angry Rurik. What they were looking for was not easily identifiable, so I knew it might take a while. The house looked smaller than the other house's interiors, even though the place had very little in it. It was surprisingly devoid of any furniture or clutter, which made our job a lot easier. "Start with the basement," I told them.

By the door lay a pile of shoes. Upon closer inspection, I had Johnson bag a muddy pair of boots. Upstairs, we found surveillance equipment, including cameras, infrared lenses, long distance recorder listening devices, a telescope, and binoculars. These were all next to the window closest to Liza's house. Other than that, we searched every corner and hidey hole, seizing his computers (which thankfully were listed in the warrant, nam-

ing one of his suspected crimes as "voyeurism)."
Eventually we heard a holler from the pair downstairs. We went down into the musty basement
where the officers had forced open a locked door
behind some shelving. Inside, a table stood covered
in small electronic parts, postage stamps, eight
monitors with different still images of the inside
of Liza's house, and finally, "The airplane!" I pro-
claimed triumphantly.

"Looks like we got more than enough evidence
to put this scumbag away," said Johnson, stroking
his beard. He was stooped over in the oppressively
small room, which his bulk took up the bulk of.

"Yes, and if he has the airplane, he might have
footage from the day Hazel died."

Johnson's eyes widened, "Wouldn't that be
neat?"

As we exited the house and Rurik was officially
placed under arrest, I spotted Liza and Mrs. McK-
raney standing on the corner watching the com-
motion. We met halfway, center lawn. "We got
him, Liza. The case is solved, and you should be
safe from this pervert now."

"About time," said Mrs. McKraney.

Liza was more appreciative. "Thank you!

Thank you so much." She went in for a handshake but wound up giving me a hug.

"Try not to thank me yet, I was promised a dinner."

She smiled, then frowned. "But what about everything you said about this having to do with my grandma? Is that what happened?"

"We know they worked at the same company. I can still talk to their coworkers after I track them down. Hopefully he will be forthcoming, and the police can get more information out of him. If we are lucky, he might rat on one of his higher-ups at Truskol, who I suspect may have had a hand in this."

"I do feel a lot better about this whole thing," said Liza. "You did a great job."

"I will go to the station with them and we'll see what we can find on the hard drives. I need to question him also, see what I can find out."

"What do you want to eat when you're done?" Liza inquired.

"Italian."

CHAPTER XIII

THE YEAR 2076

Growing up in the United States, Nigel had been to the city of Portland, Maine once before, early in his youth. He remembered it as a quiet, sleepy fishing town, filled with brick and cobblestone, the seagulls making more noise than the cars and people. Once the plane had landed, he could see firsthand that the city had changed. After the global temperatures began to climb, Americans moved en masse to the colder states. They were less prone to violent heatwaves, droughts, and storms. States which relied on livestock began to fail, but Maine and its lobsters were doing just fine. As a result of all this, Portland had become a crowded, stinking city just like any other, filled to the brim with rude people and crumbling infrastructure as a result of overpopulation and increased urbanization. It was filled with the kind of people who were willing to abandon their declining state governments for a fairer climate but would never leave the country because of their undying "patriotism."

Navigating through obnoxiously dense crowds of people, Nigel came to the address listed on the website. The building was close to the waterfront, squeezed between two newly constructed buildings of more modern architectural design. The sign swinging slowly from a rod jutting above the front window read simply, *Private Guys Private Eyes. Nate and Sam Private Investigations.*

Not wasting any time, Nigel went in through the creaky wooden door, a bell ringing to announce his entry. There was no one inside but a round, older gentleman who seemed thoroughly enraptured by his buttery lobster roll. He looked up as Nigel walked in, and after several attempts at speaking, voraciously chewed, then gulped down the rest of his sandwich. "Hiya, there! Need a detective?" he said at last.

The place was small and existed on the verge of antiquity. Looking around Nigel disappointedly accepted the fact that he would probably not receive the information he sought. "Yeah, I'm looking for detective Nathan. You him?"

The man grew older as he put down his sandwich. "No, I'm afraid Nate passed earlier this year. I'm Sam, his partner. I run the business now."

"What did him in?"

"Old age, really. He was ninety years old, drank every day, and hated doctors."

"Well, shit," Nigel snapped. "I mean, sorry and everything, but I needed some info about one of the cases he worked on. Would have been a while back."

With a bit of pride, Sam said, "Which one? Maybe I can help. I've been here since 2013 when I was just nineteen, so I'm sure I can help."

"Ever heard of Rurik Kuznetsov? News report says your buddy Nate brought him in for spying on his neighbor. Well I'm working a case for the UN and I can't find any info on this guy. All his records were disappeared."

Sam paused, then a light came into his eyes and he said, "Right, of course, yeah! That was one of Nate's favorite cases. Practically solved it in a weekend. That's where he met his wife Liza, too." Sam rose, taking his lobster roll with him. "Come back here with me, I'll let you read his notes from the case. He might have some pictures too."

"I'd rather just take them with me."

"Some of them are handwritten; it'll take me a while to dig them out. Do you want some lemonade?"

"I'm good."

They went into a cramped back room filled with old computers and filing cabinets. A musty office chair in light disrepair sat alone in a vast sea of preserved information. Sam bade Nigel to sit in the chair which groaned for a moment in protest, unused to doing its job. Sam put a monitor in front of Nigel that was so old the fact that it turned on was a true miracle. "What was the month?" Sam asked. "Never mind, I think I remember." Sam did a quick search and pulled up Nate's notes about the case. "I'll go find the rest of the notes. I think his notepad is around here somewhere..." Sam walked off mumbling to himself. Nigel began reading the first entry. It was extremely entertaining. It began: *Her legs went up to the ceiling, and so did her problems.*

CHAPTER XIV

THE YEAR 2016

Downtown, Rurik was shoved into an interrogation room and we let him wait there a while. While he was left alone to sweat it out, we grabbed some coffee down the hall. Unfortunately for everyone, the place was hot, and the air conditioner was probably broken again.

Johnson gulped his coffee, somehow immune to the effects of a burnt tongue. "We'll see if this guy has anything else in his file."

"I doubt it. Might be something on his record from Russia though."

"Welp—" Johnson gave me a monstrous elbow, causing me to spill some coffee. "Look alive, here comes the chief."

The little man marched over, chewing on a cigar, completely dwarfed in the shadow of Johnson's immensity. "Mornin' chief," said Johnson, putting down his coffee cup.

"Nathan." said Chief Henry, trying his best to look intense. "Why are you coming in here spilling the department's coffee on the floor? That's tax-payer money, comes outta our budget."

I dropped a napkin on the floor, wiping it around with my shoe, not breaking eye contact. "Would it help your beard untangle if I told you I brought in another bad guy for you?"

"Real creep," added Johnson. "Russian too."

The chief pointed a stubby finger at Johnson, like a toddler would before throwing a tantrum. "Hey, watch that shit. I'm a quarter Russian on my mother's side."

"Nevertheless," I said.

"Nevertheless, you better have enough to put him away."

"We have more than enough, Henry," I replied.

"Good. Less trash on the streets and less you in my department. He took the coffee cup from my hands and put it down on the table. "You shoulda kept your badge if you wanted the coffee." And with that, he started walking off.

"Until next time '*Chief*.'" I had to raise my voice to make sure the back of his head heard the last part. "If that's even your real name!"

I grabbed my coffee and asked Johnson, "Am I good to go in?"

He shrugged. "Sure."

"You coming with?"

He checked his watch. "Why not."

I closed the door to the interrogation room and slapped a meaningless file folder on the metal table in front of the handcuffed Rurik. He was sweating from the heat, and the florescent light shone brightly off the slick, empty patch left by his receding hairline. Johnson stood in the corner of the room, a stolid, motionless gargoyle. As I pulled up a chair in front of him, Rurik scowled harder, the lines in his face growing, serving only to make him look older. He was hunched forward in his chair, keeping his eyes fixed on the table.

"Rurik Kuznetsov," I said. "Or do you prefer Angelo?"

He remained silent.

"I will call you Rurik. We found a lot of stuff in that basement Rurik. Care to explain?"

He remained silent.

"The cold-shoulder, huh? Is that why you came to Florida? Russia was too cold for you?" I flipped through the file, pretending to find it engrossing. "Why were you so interested in your neighbor there, Rurik?" I shrugged my shoulders mockingly, "Had a crush on her? I can understand that. But breaking in? We found a model plane in your basement; Liza says that belongs to her. Did you steal the plane when you broke in? Is that what you wanted?"

Rurik glanced up for an instant, long enough for me to notice. He remained silent.

"Look Rurik, this is just a conversation. I just want to understand why you were spying on Liza, that is all. Just level with me, and this will all go a lot easier for you, I promise."

He remained silent.

I began flipping through the file intently, stopping in a random spot and pointing to it. "Yeah, okay. So here it says you worked at the same company as Liza's grandmother. Is that true? You must have known her."

He shifted uncomfortably in his chair, remaining silent.

"But you knew she passed away, right? Did you go to the funeral?" It may have just been me, but he seemed to scowl harder. He remained silent.

Johnson jumped in, remaining stiffly in the corner with his arms crossed. His voice hit a baritone. "Look guy. He's tryin' to help you. But if you don't start answerin' some questions, we'll tell 'em you were uncooperative. This will all be much harder, and you'll be in the can much longer, that's for sure. I seen it a million times with cocky scum like you."

I raised my eyebrows at Rurik, nodding. He seemed unfazed. "Maybe you had a crush on Hazel huh? Why stalk her granddaughter then?" Nothing. The man was a brick wall. "Okay, okay. I am making too many assumptions, huh? Maybe she wronged you, you wanted a little payback. I can understand that. Or maybe, maybe she stole something from you. Something you needed back but did not want the police's help with."

He sniffed and remained silent.

"You have a right to property in this country. You probably learned about that when you got your citizenship. John Locke's idea. If that was the case, maybe we could have it returned to you. Maybe a jury or a judge would look more favorably on a situation like that."

As he remained silent, his stoicism began to speak volumes.

Johnson interjected once more. "Or maybe, he's just a perverted piece of trash who gets off on bein' a creep. They won't look too 'favorably' on that will they?"

Looking at Rurik, I pushed my eyebrows together and shook my head. He acknowledged nothing. We sat there in complete silence for three minutes, nobody moving. Except me. I drank my coffee.

Finally, I offered up my own personal theory. "Or maybe, maybe, it had something to do with your work. Maybe you were jealous of something she did. Or, even better, maybe this is not your fault at all. Maybe she took something she was not supposed to, something, I don't know, proprietary? Maybe it was your job to bring it back. Maybe, if you told us who was up there giving you the instructions, we can get you off the hook.

Right partner?" I looked up at Johnson who shrugged.

Rurik craned his neck sideways, rubbing his head on his shoulder to wipe up some of the sweat that was pouring down and stinging his eyes. I saw the edge of his shirt vibrating and could tell that he was repetitively and violently pumping his leg under the table.

I grinned politely, closing the file. "And maybe it has something to do with Hazel's notes. Her diagrams and hard drives which she kept in that big metal box."

Rurik stirred, starting to stutter. "I—I—"

"And maybe that is why you tried to break into my office. You thought I had it there? No sir, that is in evidence now, right partner?" Johnson nodded, probably having no idea what I was talking about.

Rurik's eyes darted between us, his sweat dripping onto the table. "I want a lawyer!"

I threw up my hands. "Fine, you can have a lawyer, but that will be the end of our friendly conversation. However, if you give us names and we continue our conversation, most of this can go away. You will be out in no time."

Johnson said, "And if you don't you'll be rottin' the rest of yer natural life while they're vacationing in Hawaii."

"Are you sure that is what you want?" I asked. He hesitated. "Who at Truskol wanted that info?"

There was a knock at the door. Johnson made a swift exit. A few seconds later, he opened the door again and beckoned me, "Nate."

I left Rurik in the stuffy room with its metal table and asked Johnson the obvious question.

"It's that Hazel lady. They found the video," he answered.

We went down the hall to a room filled with servers and monitors. Thankfully, it seemed to have its own air-conditioning system, sperate from the rest of the building's. A detective was going over the evidence we brought in from Rurik's house. He was responsible for running all the software forensics for the department.

He played a section of a video from inside the house. Its perspective was just above eye-level, probably in the living room. It was recorded during the daytime, and I was told the video had no sound. A man with a ski mask, gloves and a collapsible knife walked into frame, and started rummaging through kitchen drawers. He wore the same muddy boots I had spotted at Rurik's house. He looked up suddenly, as if he heard a noise, and ran behind the couch at full speed, hiding just as the front door opened and a smartly dressed older woman stepped through. She took off her shoes and closed the door. She walked toward the closet to put something away and noticed something was amiss when she saw something peeking out from behind her couch.

She backed up slowly, putting her bag down, and tipping off the intruder. She screamed with a look of absolute terror as the man popped out and advanced toward her. She ran, managing to make it to the front door, opening it before the man came up from behind and grabbed her, pulling her back. She struggled, and he threw her down, knocking her into the kitchen chairs. She fell hard, and began to try and get up, when she clutched her chest and slumped back down, agony splashed across her features. The intruder was upon her once more, but realizing something was wrong, stepped back. She lay upon the floor, now motionless. Panicking, the man looked around frantically, ran toward the camera, picked it up, and started moving toward the backdoor. He covered the camera lens with his hand, so that everything was now black.

The detective stopped the playback.

I gave a long and much needed sigh. "Well, shit."

"That 'bout what you expected?" asked Johnson.

"Kind of. That about ties things up at least."

After Rurik's lawyer arrived, we presented him with the video evidence, to which he only bowed his head shamefully.

"This is you, right?" I asked.

His lawyer instructed him not to answer.

"What were you looking for? The box?"

"You need to give us somethin,'" added Johnson. "We've got everthin' we need. It's just a matter of explainin' yourself."

The lawyer whispered something in Rurik's ear, covering her mouth with a piece of paper. And in that moment, looking at Rurik's sweaty downcast features, I had a realization. "You do not work for Truskol, do you?" He lifted his head, startled. I kept going. "Look, you obviously did not mean to kill her. If you tell us who put you up to this and you cooperate, that will be taken into consideration.

"It was me," he said hoarsely, much to the chagrin of his lawyer, who had her thumb on her temple to rub her forehead, her eyes tightly shut. Rurik continued, "No one else. Just me. I have nothing else to say."

I left the interrogation room in the hopes of a less stuffy environment that might provide a cool breeze or a draft of air, which would alleviate the overwhelming discomfort that only a completely sweaty body can afford. But if anything, the outside of the room was even hotter and stuffier, probably from all the sweaty cops who were running around generating their own tiny sources of heat. "Can one of you guys crack a window?" I yelled. No one paid me any mind.

"Whatcha gonna do now?" asked Johnson, coming up from behind.

"I want to learn more about Truskol and the part they played in all this."

"But didn't ya hear him? He said it was just him, nobody else." Johnson suggested, laughing.

"And I'm seeing Liza tonight. I should tell her about what happened to her grandmother."

"That's probably a good idea. She should know. Just keep the details light, y'know?"

"Yeah, yeah, I don't think it will jeopardize the conviction, but sure. She will probably have to testify after all."

"Speaking of which, you're not really keeping a big box of evidence, are you?"

"No, I was just lying to him. I don't have anything like that."

"Hm."

"Well, you keep working on him, I doubt we will get much more though."

"Alright Nate, see you later."

I left the station and got to work.

CHAPTER XV

THE YEAR 2076

The sky was beginning to darken, causing the room to become ever more claustrophobic. Nigel had been reading for a few hours now and had sent Sam out to buy him some food. He read the last page from Nathan Gallup's account of the case and turned off the monitor.

He went back out to the front of the office and waited at the front desk for Sam's return. While he waited, a call came through on Nigel's international phone. "Nigel? It's Frank."

"Frank," said Nigel.

"Nigel," said Frank. "I been looking into Rurik. At first, I couldn't find anything. But I went deeper, climbed a little higher up the food chain.

Your guy Rurik was a Russian agent. Maybe a full spy, maybe not. He'd been working in America for a while. But yeah, that's all I got. Literally, I couldn't find anything else. Not even how long he was there or when he came back."

Nigel let out a long, low whistle. "That explains why his info was wiped clean. The Russian government probably had him smuggled out of the US too."

"Now about the plane ride—" Frank was cut off.

"Whoops, gotta go. Bye!" Nigel hastily ended the call.

Sitting in silence in the darkening room, Nigel began to piece things together. And he knew exactly where he needed to go next. Eventually, Sam walked in carrying a cloth sack. "I grabbed two different kinds, I figured I'd eat whichever one you didn't want."

"I'll take it with me."

Sam looked a little crestfallen. Clearly, he did not have many lunch companions. "So, did you get what you needed?"

"Yes, I did. I have a good picture of what happened to my murdered guy. What I don't know is why. You said Nate married Liza, his client from that case, right?"

"Yes. The last time I saw her was at the funeral."

"Where's she?"

"She's right here in Portland. They moved with the business."

Nigel grabbed the food from Sam. "Good job old-timer. Makin' my life easier. You get a gold star."

After receiving Liza's address, Nigel took a maglev train across the city to her house, making it there in no time at all. Luckily for him, the case was progressing quickly. He came to a quaint, two-story home with bright-blue vinyl siding and an impressive oak tree standing guard. A robot the size of a pie was hard at work trimming the lawn. He walked up to the front door, which opened before he could do much more than that.

A woman in her early nineties stood in front of Nigel, dressed smartly, ready for a gallery opening or business meeting. "Hi Detective Woods. Sam called ahead and told me you were coming."

"I'll get straight to the point then... Liza." She said nothing, implying that he was right to assume it was she.

"Come in," she said, gesturing.

Nigel entered the home, which was clean, yet filled with a lifetime of memories. The walls were lavender and the carpet, a pale yellow, a color which Liza's hair mysteriously still maintained. The couch was the blue of the Caribbean, and as inviting as the rest of the home. As far as Nigel could tell, they were the only two in the house.

"Anything to drink?" Liza asked.

"I'm good."

Liza sat down on the sofa. Nigel remained standing. "Do you remember the man who was spying on you in 2016 when you first met your husband? Your neighbor in Florida at the time."

"Of course. It's when we first met. He'd said his name was Angelo, but it was—"

"Rurik?" Nigel suggested.

"That's right. Nate thought he wanted something from my grandmother."

"Right, they had worked together at..." Nigel looked down, then back up. "...Truskol Energy. Did he ever figure out what that was about?"

"No. Nate kept looking into it, but he didn't get very far. And when Rurik left the country, that was pretty much the end of it."

"And did Nate ever figure out what your grand-mother was trying to hide in her notes?"

Liza put both her hands on the seat of the couch. "How did you know about that?"

"I read Nate's journal of the case. So, what of it?"

Liza gave him a wary look but continued. "No one could ever figure out what they were. Maybe it's best that way. Why are you here, might I ask?"

"I'm a detective with the UN. The man who stalked you, Rurik, I just pulled his prints off a knife I found at my murder scene."

Her eyes grew wide. "Here? In the US?"

"No, it looks like he went back to his native Russia, then hopped a boat to an outpost in Antarctica. I'm just trying to get a clear picture of what happened."

"It's just you?"

Nigel scratched the back of his head. "Because of the recent, uh, global troubles, more countries are asking us to step in, which means my department's getting bigger. Not fast enough though. Which is why I need to wrap this up quickly. Now I know it was a long time ago, but can you give me any description of the guy? Any birthmarks or anything? I can't find anything in his file."

"No, not really, I hardly saw him. He seemed like kind of a pale, greasy man."

"Okay, well, exactly how old was he? Do you remember?"

Liza paused to think, playing with the frills on one of the couch's pillows. "He was definitely over forty. Middle ages, I'd say. Older than Nate and I."

Nigel slowly sat down on the blue loveseat by the couch. "Ohhhh... shit. Wait. Oh, shit."

"What?"

"I know what happened." Nigel sat without speaking for a few minutes. Liza may have said something, maybe not. Then, he quickly stood back up. "Do you still have that box with your grandmother's notes?"

"No, but we brought it back to the Florida house after the hurricane came through and destroyed the business. The box was fine, just a little dented."

"So, it's still in Florida?"

"Yeah."

"Is there any way I can get my hands on it?"

"Um, I don't know. I guess I could let you in. What do you need it for?"

"Evidence."

"Well, okay. At my age, I don't think I'll be going back down there again anyway. As long as I get some kind of receipt or something from your superiors."

"Sure, sure, whatever you want. Do you have the key?"

"If you guys tell me when you're at the house, I can unlock it from here."

"Okay. I'll make a couple calls, have my boss contact you directly, and I'll head straight there."

He left the house and stood out front. He tried to get a message through to Oslow but there was interference and he could not be reached. *Terrific, another storm,* Nigel surmised.

"Janice," said Nigel, video calling from his wrist display while on Liza's front lawn.

"What now?" asked Janice, clearly busy doing something unseemly with someone's dead body.

"Get Tom."

"Not my job!"

"If I said please, would you do it?"

She gave him a sideways look, then went back to

her work. "Saying, 'If I say please,' does not count as saying 'please.'"

Nigel drew a long, slow breath. "Ple-ase."

"What was that?" Janice asked, not turning from her work.

"Just go get him!"

"Fine!" she threw down her gloves and stormed off.

Just when Nigel began questioning whether she had simply left with no intention of returning, she came back into view. "He's on." She clicked a button and the image changed to one of a blonde man with no shirt and a hairy chest. "Tom," Nigel said. "Um, your shirt?"

"You interrupted me. What do you want?"

"I want you to put on a shirt. This lady needs to talk to Boss Tom."

"Ugh, why? Haven't we talked about this?"

"Can you just talk to her? I need some evidence from her. She wants to make sure it's logged, that's all."

"You couldn't just—"

"Time-sensitive stuff, Tom. Come on man, just put on a shirt."

"Ugh." Tom pulled a dress shirt from his desk

drawer and put it on. "You'd better close this one Nigel, or I'll have your badge."

Nigel waved him off. "Yeah, yeah. I'm handing you over now."

After Liza sorted everything with Nigel's superiors, he once again boarded his plane and flew to Florida. He landed it in an empty airstrip, since the airport nearest Liza's house was abandoned. Most of the city, most of the state, had been vacated by the locals or decimated by tropical storms. Nigel stepped off the plane wearing a T-shirt and jeans, then immediately jumped back in and changed into a tank top and short shorts. While changing, he asked the automatic pilot, "Jesus! What's the temperature?"

"The surrounding temperature of the plane is just over one hundred and thirty-two-degrees Fahrenheit," replied the plane's disembodied voice. "It is suggested that you take water on your excursion."

"Yeah thanks, I'll be fine."

Nigel ordered a self-driving car which was a tiny, slow-moving thing, probably powered by potatoes or something. It drove straight up to the plane, and Nigel stuffed himself inside. He was driven through a veritable ghost town of empty streets, closed down businesses, and sadness. When they arrived at their destination, an out of the way dead-end street surrounded by the withering husks of trees, the car turned itself off and unfurled a solar map from its roof that hung out over the edges of the car.

Walking up to what he assumed to be the correct house, Nigel saw holographic notices displayed on the front of every door in the neighborhood. All the houses seemed to be abandoned, and each one had a notice. The one on Liza's door read:

NOTICE:

NEIGHBORHOOD POWER GRID

WILL BE TURNED OFF

EFFECTIVE APRIL 7TH

FOR MORE INFORMATION VISIT

FLORIDA   DISTRICT   RENEWABLE POWER

OFFICE 73

Oh, that's just wonderful. Despite the sign, when Nigel walked in after contacting Liza, he was greeted by a blast of cool air, as if kissed by an angel. And although he could feel the air conditioning running, it was an apparently silent process. The house was conspicuously devoid of furniture, but some pieces remained. They were mostly big things like the couch and the bedframes. Likewise, the old-timey kitchen appliances remained but were unplugged. The only other items in the house were boxed up and neatly organized, their contents labeled for ease of access. Making his way upstairs, Nigel turned into the study, switched on the light, and began his search for a box marked *Files, Miscellaneous*. Liza had said she was not exactly sure where her husband had left it, but it was definitely in that room. Maybe.

When he had come to the brink of giving in, a panel behind the other boxes in the closet slid out to reveal the metal box described in Nate's recounting of his experience. Nigel forced it open, to make sure he was not, in fact, leaving emptyhanded, and was relieved to find Hazel's notes inside.

Before leaving, Nigel tried Oslow one more time, but to no avail. He took his autonomous taxi back to the jet, thankful to be leaving that godforsaken place. The transitions from sweltering to cool were making him nauseated. On the plane, he looked through the box, registering nothing but incomprehensible symbols. Checking the amount of time that had elapsed since his Antarctic departure, he knew it would be a short trip to UN headquarters in New York, and he decided to fly there first, dump the box off, then fly back to Antarctica.

On the way, he used UN resources to dig a little deeper into Truskol Energy Corporation. Truskol had been investigated several times for practicing both corporate and economic espionage, either aided by or under the direction of the Russian government. In the end, while under investigation, the company stopped doing business in America altogether, eventually closing its doors completely. There was not much more information since nothing was ever proven, but if Rurik were an agent of the Russian government, his "job" at Truskol may have only served to obfuscate his activities.

In any case, Nigel arrived at United Nations headquarters. It was composed of a gated office park which radiated around a central tower so tall and polished, it was a hazard to low-flying aircraft and birds of all kinds. But that was a small sacrifice to be made for the world's last true beacon of hope.

The plane taxied into its hangar and came to a stop. Nigel leapt out and as quickly as possible, navigated the maze of office buildings, floors, departments, and security checks, finally making his way to the head honchos' offices, box in tow. Nigel, walking with purpose, spotted Tom heading downstairs, away from his desk, and sped up dramatically, almost tripping on the carpet. "Yo Tom!" Nigel's boss, who was very much within earshot, did not turn. Tom was a reasonably athletic man and never walked slowly if he could help it. He continued calmly on his way. "Tom!" Nigel started gaining but was slowed considerably by the heavy metal box he had half tucked under his arm.

Finally, in front of the elevator, Nigel caught up with Tom. Tom spun on him. "What is it? Do you have a murderer for me or what? There are other cases piling up as we speak."

"You'll want to keep me on this one," said Nigel, patting the metal box. "I need this brought down to the research department and popped open ASAP, no delays, no filing. I need to know what this is."

Tom grabbed the box with his rough hands, trying to open it. "Why?"

As people walked by, he popped it open and Nigel shoved out a swift hand, closing it right back up. "The Russians are after it like you wouldn't believe. Just get it down there for me. It's maybe something nuclear, but it's coded so we might need a codebreaker or a program to crack it, if we have any."

"Not much use then, is it?"

"I can help with that. But until then, let me know if there is anything they can figure out."

"And where are you going?"

"I'm taking a couple meatheads to catch your murderer." And so, he did.

CHAPTER XVI

THE YEAR 2076

Nigel took four trained peacekeepers with him, back to his plane. They were trained security personnel, experienced in making arrests and dealing with various threats. However, their main job was to protect UN employees in dangerous parts of the world. Nigel gave them a briefing once everyone was onboard. He stood at the front of the jet to address the UN officers who, all four, looked uncomfortable. They were fully armored and geared up, squished together in the small cabin. "Listen up, meatheads, this'll take a while, so get comfy. The trip is a couple hours, then you have to wait in here for my signal. Do NOT leave the cabin until I give the word. Understand?" Nigel looked around. No one said anything. "Do you underr-ssstand-uh?"

They all nodded. One raised his hand and asked, "Yes sir, but how long are we waiting in the plane?"

"Until I give the signal. Could be ten minutes, could be ten hours. You get paid either way. I have some illegal stuff to do first, then you can come in." The officers glanced at each other. "When I tell you to, all you have to do is meet me at my location, should be the main building, and arrest who I'm pointing at. Got it?" There were some mumbles that Nigel took to mean yes. So, he charted their course (which means he quietly told the ship to take him back to Antarctica) and they were on their way.

The first thing Nigel did when he returned to the base was find Oslow. Not having been able to get in touch with him, Nigel hoped the strange little man was still intact. Indeed, he was, Nigel learned, when he found Oslow resting inside the staff quarters building. "Yo Ozzy!" Nigel's voice was raised in order to awaken Oslow, who appeared to be dozing.

Surprised, Oslow started, then fell from his

bunk with a vicious thud. He spoke fervent, frustrated words in Russian, readjusted his belongings that had fallen, then, finding his translator, turned it on. "Detective, you startled me. You were gone for a long while. Did you find anything?"

Nigel chose his words carefully. "I might have something. I couldn't get ahold of you. Was there a storm or something?"

"A small one, but it passed quickly,"

"Have you seen Catherine?" Nigel asked.

"Not recently, no. But she was asking where you had gone. Do you need me to find her?"

"Not right now, just make sure you two are ready. I'll need her later when I wrap up this stupid case."

"Oslow's eyes lit up. You have it solved?"

Nigel ignored him. "What time is it?"

"Well, um, just after midnight."

"Place'll be closing in a bit, right?"

"The research building, yes."

"Okay. I need to find Carl. He's not working right now, is he?"

"I don't know. I don't think so."

"Come on Oz, step it up. Stop sleeping on the job." With those words, Nigel left the room before

Oslow could respond. Outside, it was as cold as it had ever been, but the wind and the snow had subsided, leaving the miles of barren landscape dead quiet. The quiet was only exacerbated by crisp, inky blackness, somehow more real than the hazy glare of day.

Making his way through the housing village, Nigel found Carl's shelter after more than one attempt. It did not escape Nigel's notice that the hole he had kicked in Carl's miniature snow fortress had been carefully repaired. *How do these people have time to do any actual work?* Nigel knocked. Living up to expectations, Carl did not answer. Nigel knocked again, this time yelling, "Carl! You're under arrest! I got four guys standing here, more than happy to break your flimsy door down."

Immediately, the door burst opened, "What the bloody hell are you on about?" Carl was glancing around like a madman, looking for armed guards.

Nigel smiled wide, "There he is." With a shocking abruptness, Nigel managed to both push and squirm past Carl, successfully forcing himself through the narrow doorway. "Nice digs you got here, all to yourself I see."

Carl whirled around; his face contorted into

a hardly recognizable version of its former self. "What are—get the—"

Nigel sat himself calmly down in a small folding chair at the foot of Carl's bed. He basked under overhead heat lamps, throwing his cumbersome coat on the floor. "We need to talk about who killed Anton."

Carl looked down at Nigel, Carl's face the hue of something unpleasant. "And what, you think I did it?"

"No, not at all. I just needed you to open a door. But I know who did."

Carl glanced around outside, closed the door, then crossed his arms. "Fine, you have five minutes. What do you want from me?"

Nigel leaned the chair back precipitously, trying to make himself more comfortable. It wobbled defiantly, and he leaned it forward again, deciding against that course of action's furtherance. "Do you have any idea why the widow Minsky told me I should talk to you when I asked her about her husband's death?"

Carl swallowed painfully. His body swayed and shifted, becoming perfectly still again, as if he made up his mind to sit down, then immediately decided against it. "I have no idea. I didn't know—"

"How often was he in here?" Nigel asked, dramatically looking around the room. "Every night? Once a week?"

"I—I don't—"

"How often was Anton coming in here to see you?"

Carl bowed his head. He slowly shuffled over to the bed, deciding to sit down after all. "Whenever he could. Without getting caught." Then Carl looked up at Nigel with a sense of urgency, his eyes watering. "But we didn't have anything to do with his death. Her or me. I, I thought she didn't know. She told you?"

"I think she had a pretty good idea. But why don't you give me a little more, so I have all the facts straight."

Carl cast his eyes back down. "When we were at Oxford, that's when I met Anton. But he was already engaged to Nina. So, I was with him in England, and she saw him when he went back to Russia during the breaks. She had just graduated. He went through with the marriage, but I didn't give up on him. He'd been offered a job here as an engineer, and we decided to come, so it would be easier to see each other. It sort of worked... for a while."

Nigel was pleased with himself. "And the knife you checked out, that was a favor for him, wasn't it? Anton mysteriously lost it, didn't he?"

"Carl, whose cheeks had become moist, looked absolutely dumbfounded. "Yeah, how did you know?"

"Because I don't believe in coincidence. By the way, that Ivan guy, at the quartermaster's station. He a friend of yours? He seemed reluctant to sell you out."

"He's an alright bloke. Anton and I would hang around and give him grief. I don't know anything past that though. He's a bit gormless if you ask me."

Nigel leaned over, digging around in his coat on the floor. He pulled out the list Ivan had given him. "I think this might be the reason," he said. "I was takin' a look at some of these transactions. Looks like Ivan has been making money selling some extra drugs on the side. He didn't cover it up very well either. He probably just didn't want anyone digging but—"

"Look, Anton wasn't into that stuff if that's what you're getting at. Ivan's just a dodgy guy."

"Fair enough," Nigel said, putting away the list. "Let's try this thing again. When was the last time you saw Anton?"

"The day before he died. We were just getting some lunch."

"What'd you talk about?"

"I don't know, everything, nothing, the usual stuff."

Nigel grew irritated. "Carl, what was Anton doing trying to get in the building? There was no emergency maintenance call, and the place was locked down. He was off duty. Think for a minute before you start yammering again."

Carl did think, and based on his indecision before producing his response, what he thought of seemed just relevant enough to warrant mention. "I don't know. The only thing I can think of is, last week I kinda remember him talking about how the station, something about its power generators. He thought there was something wonky about where the electricity was being routed from. He said he wanted to look into it. That's the only thing I can think of."

"And why wasn't he with you the night he died?"

"He wanted some sleep. And he was kind of upset about Nina leaving."

"Was he usually sleeping around that time?"

"Yeah mate, pretty much. Everyone who works here does." Carl stood up with a nervous energy and began to pace the length of the room. "You know, I bet in whatever file you have on him, it doesn't mention that he's a sambo champion. A gold medalist in Russia. And you saw how big he is! How does someone break a man's neck like that? It doesn't make sense."

"Sambo, that's the Russian martial art?"

"One of 'em, yeah, that's right."

"Well, hopefully, you'll find out what happened soon enough. But in order to make that happen, I need your help to confirm my theory. That's why I'm here."

"Oh, bollocks, that's 'why you're here.' There's no way you knew all of that stuff I just told you before you came in here."

Nigel did nothing but sit silently with an enormous grin on his face.

Carl threw up his hands in exasperation. "You're a real smarmy arse, you know that?"

"Look, you annoying brit. Here's the skinny. All I need is that thing you use to get in the building."

Carl finally stopped pacing. "Why?

"To get in the building."

"Am I getting it back?"

"You can get another one if I lose it, right?"

"No, not really. And it'll cost me if I can get another one."

"Yes, but can you put a price on avenging your lover's brutal murder?"

Carl rolled his eyes and handed Nigel a simple and very old-fashioned little cube that would permit Nigel entry. Nigel pocketed it and asked, "What's the time?" As he did so, a holographic display card that read *12:42* popped up in front of him, then slowly faded to nothing. It was almost time. Nigel gathered up his coat, waited for the heater to kick in, and ducked out of the hut, bracing for the cold.

Out of nowhere, a blast of incompressible chill rocked the back of Nigel's head as a snowball crashed into him. "That's for my fort!" said Carl, quickly shutting the door.

Nigel pulled with all his might, trying in vain to open the door, seeking vengeance. He finally gave up, and violently dusted the snow from his hair. Then, he made his way over to the edge of that section of housing units which faced the building soon to be locking itself up for the night, protecting its precious data while its residents slept. He went inside a bar made of two combined housing units with a window cut out of the center. He sat by the window which gave him a clear view of the buildings off in the distance. He ordered a bowl of protein mush while he waited and watched everyone file out toward the snowmobiles or make their way to one of the attached structures. He looked disappointingly at the bowl of mush, then smiled heartily when he thought of the officers that he had left sitting in the plane with no one to keep them company but their own dumb selves and the snippy autopilot. He had brought them along, hiding them in the plane so no one would be tipped off by any incoming aircraft when the time was right.

After a little less than a half hour, Nigel's protein mush was gone, and the building appeared empty. The security guards were last to leave. Nigel sat tight for another half hour or so, avoiding eye contact with the barkeep, then left. He walked the full way in the dark to the building, leaving his snowmobile behind. Nigel trudged toward the bright lights of the research base. It was an unbearably slow trek, and the longer he walked, the colder he became. Eventually, when he had barely made it halfway, Nigel was forced to turn his coat's heater up to its maximum setting. During a storm, it would have been impossible to see him walking toward the buildings. But as it was, Nigel knew he was in plain view of anyone who might be paying close enough attention. That person might have wondered to his or herself what exactly Nigel was thinking, making the long walk, alone in the freezing cold. Nigel was beginning to wonder the same thing.

After an eternity had passed, Nigel finally arrived at his destination. He had, to the best of his knowledge, retraced Anton's path from the night of his demise. Nigel eagerly approached the backdoor of the facility where the crime had allegedly taken place. He put the entry cube Carl had given him up to the scanner, to open the door. The door did not open. He tried it several more times, cursing all the while. The almost illegibly small screen on the side of the door displayed no words and emitted no sound. He looked around, then looked behind him at the distance he had travelled. Afraid he might actually freeze to death if he attempted a return trip, he flung out his arm, trying the door one more time. Expectedly, the door did not open. Yet Nigel paused. On the last attempt, he heard a faint noise which he had failed to notice on his earlier tries. He was perfectly silent, only moving his hand, putting the cube in front of the door's scanner once more. This time, he was sure he heard a low mechanical click, as if the door were unlocking. It was as if it were trying to open but failed to do so.

Nigel looked directly above him at the overhang and its single, blindingly bright bulb. It was an archaic mechanism, a simple light emitting diode surrounded by glass. He smashed it. And when he did, all became darkness on that secluded section of snow behind the facility. He stooped a little, huddling closer to the metal door and letting his eyes adjust for a moment. A thin, unwavering sliver of crimson light was visible, streaming from the edge of the door where it was supposed to meet its place in the frame. *Well, well...*

A ridiculous looking smile spread across Nigel's face as he presented the cube for scanning once more. The sliver of light widened ever so slightly, as the door made a clinking, knocking sound. *Anton, you clever old so, and so,* thought Nigel. He grabbed the door by its manual service handle and heaved and hoed, widening the crack between the door and the wall just enough for him to slip a gloved hand through, and push with all his being. The door slid completely open, grinding and whirring all the while, then shut silently once Nigel stepped through and let it go.

Looking around, Nigel found himself back where his hellish adventure had first begun. He was in the round storage room with the huge ventilation pipes, the room just through the corridor and past the main entrance. He was happy to be back indoors, but with only the dim red emergency lights to show him the way, the whole vibe was deeply unsettling. He made his way as quickly and quietly as he could possibly manage, desperate not to set off any alarms. He became lost as he once had while looking for the doctor, but purposefully this time.

Navigating the maze of cramped hallways, he recognized the mysterious room with its cameras, this time, bathed in red and absent any guards. He stepped closer, avoiding the cameras as best he could (or the ones he could see anyway). And the further he progressed toward the door, the louder the pounding in his chest became, until it was a dull roaring, thumping—

That's not me, thought Nigel. *It's coming from in there.*

He was as close as he could be to the door, without the cameras spotting him. He stood behind a support beam, alone in the hallway, listening intently. The thudding, rumbling noise was so deep and dull, it seemed halfway outside the range of human hearing. In fact, if Nigel stood still enough, he was sure he could feel it vibrating the floor, through the soles of his boots, right up his legs.

Finally, he thought, *What the hell,* threw his coat's hood over his face, made a beeline for the door and...

It did not open. He tugged at it a few times, then rushed back behind cover. Nigel looked around, confused, surveying his environment with fresh eyes and new purpose. *C'mon Anton. How?* Nigel noticed thick ventilation tubes along the ceiling that originated from the side of the hallway whence he came. They led into the mysterious locked room through the wall above the door. Nigel gleefully snapped his fingers, which made no noise since he was still wearing gloves. He ran back to the storage room where he had come in, following the ceiling's ventilation tubes all the way.

Now Nigel had a new problem. He needed to access the ventilation tubes which were twenty feet up from the floor. There were no ladders in the room. Nigel came across a box of blue safety harnesses which attached to the ceiling via a simple rope and pulley system. *Um, no.* Aside from his not knowing how to use the harnesses, the biggest problem was that even if he used them, or even a rickety stack of boxes, or a ladder for that matter, someone walking by would know he was up there, while he was sneaking into a place where he clearly should not be. He searched for any other means of reaching the ventilation system and wondered if there was a hover seat onboard the plane. *Probably not. No time anyway.*

Finally, he settled on the worst possible option: a simple rope, a coil of cable lying under a toolbox. To one end, he tied his boot. To the other, with a bowline knot, his waist. Fortunately, the tube he needed was close to the wall, so he could kick off it once he started climbing. It was also (hopefully) large enough to support a man. Nigel threw the boot with the cable attached and threw it hard. It thunked into the side of the hollow tube and fell to the ground, making a raucous clamor. Instinctively, Nigel glanced around, but all remained silent. He tried twice more, each time with more finesse, finally slinging the shoe all the way around the tube on his third attempt. He tied the shoe around the side of the cable he was holding, then pulled it, tightening the rope around the tube. He climbed up, kicking off the wall as best he could. When he came to the top, he perched on the wide tube, straddling it for dear life. He pulled up the cord and shoe, untied them, and, coiling the cord, put the coil inside his coat. Inspecting the ventilation system, he found a panel near the far end of the tube, by the door, that, if it were to come off, would be large enough for him to wriggle inside. Carefully, Nigel shimmied backward toward it, pushing with his hands and hips, while still straddling the pipe. It was most undignified.

Reaching the access panel, he pulled out a multi-tool to unscrew it, but the screws were already missing. He popped the panel out and stretched uncomfortably far to place it on a metal box attached to the wall. He slid/dropped/ squeezed inside the pipe. It was just as dusty and horrible and cramped as he had imagined, and it was then that he realized with horrifying clarity that the coffin sized pipe might actually be his tomb. He crawled forward. Luckily, the tube was made of rigid plastic that had a little bit of give, so he did not make as much noise awkwardly shuffling through as he thought he would. Every couple of meters, a small bit of red light shined through an access panel, and it was just enough light to see by.

For Nigel, it was slow going at first, but he gradually developed a kind of rhythm that allowed him to move forward, inch by inch, as efficiently as possible. He was able to wear his thick coat inside the tube, but anyone larger than he would not have been able. Rounding the corner to go down the hall was especially difficult, and for a moment, unhappy memories of his childhood sprang up, ones of becoming stuck in playground slides. Before too long, he came upon another sharp turn and knew the pipe was turning into the room where he wanted to be.

As slowly and carefully as could be reasonably managed, he took the turn, looking for the nearest access panel. Squinting, he could just make one out. Where normally the panel would have a grate with slits, this panel was covered by something. It was tape maybe, or cloth. This time, Nigel need both his flashlight and his multitool to unfasten the panel. When, after some sweat and some angry mumbling, the panel finally came out, Nigel slid it slowly, inching it sideways. Nigel looked down through the man-sized hole, about half uncovered. The room, while generous in size, was almost completely empty. The steel door was apparently the only exit from the room, and it had three separate security panels connected on the wall beside it. No handle or apparent locking mechanism was visible. On the wall furthest from the door, a huge projection monitor was deactivated, showing nothing, and with no visible hardware connected to it.

But what first drew Nigel's eye as he looked

down from his perch, was not the door or monitor, but what lay alone in the exact center of the floor. It was a hatch, with a huge locking wheel attached to what Nigel could only assume was a dog lever. The wheel would have to be rotated open, then heaved directly upward in order to permit entry. *Oh, this is gonna suck.*

Very, very, very carefully and with great deliberation, Nigel was able to sling his shoe grappling hook all the way around the top of an adjacent and smaller tube, then catch the shoe as it swung underneath. He tied it off, and rappelled down, the cable wrapped around his arm. He was thankful for the gloves.

On ground level once more, he first tried to activate the display monitor, but had no success. Not wanting to lose more time, Nigel, through humongous bursts of strength, rotated open the hatch, and pulled it up from the floor. A set of stairs and bright lights lined a wall, leading down. Nigel took the first two steps, bending completely over to peek inside the hatch, underneath the floor. There was no one. The room in which he began to descend was smaller than the last and was filled almost entirely by a freight elevator and some empty metal shelving.

The elevator was big enough to almost fit a car, and Nigel felt like a small child as he entered. It was foolish, he knew, descending blindly unto unknown territory deep beneath the ground with only one slow method of escape, at the center of a murder plot. But it was not his first time, and probably not the last. It was a simple elevator with just two buttons for up and down, certainly not up to any sort of safety codes. Nigel, his hand hovering over the buttons, almost turned around and left, reasoning that he was not being paid enough to do something so foolish. But he pressed the button for down, remembering that he was indeed being paid enough.

After a descent that lasted almost five minutes, the elevator's doors opened. To anyone paying attention, the elevator would have seemed empty, since Nigel was hiding in the corner. He manipulated the bit of glass from the top of his wrist display, using its reflection to peek around the corner. There were metal railings and a walkway, but as far as he could tell, no people. This put him more on edge. Whatever pounding noise he had heard from above was much louder now, and Nigel doubted anyone could have heard the elevator. Unfortunately, the sound also meant that he would not be able to hear approaching footsteps.

With the swiftness of a viper, Nigel's head darted around the corner and back again. The elevator doors began to close, and he held them open. He took one more look, then rounded the corner of the elevator with a tentative step. Nigel found himself in an immense, roughly hewn cavern that might have been manmade, natural, or more probably both. There was a simple metal railing and walkway stretching straight in front of him and another met it at a right angle, stretching off to the right. On his left was a dark brown wall of rock and ice. Some small lights came up from the floor, and they did a surprisingly good job of lighting the cavern. While deep, the cavern did not extend very far, for Nigel could see the opposite wall straight in front of him. A lively jog would probably see him reach it in under a minute. Nigel stepped into the shadows, concealing himself as best he could, the floor rhythmically vibrating under his feet. Moving to the walkway that disappeared past a rocky wall to his right, he looked past the wall for a second, then ducked back behind it. In front of the elevator, he had a wide but comfortable alcove. But past it, he now knew that the walkways went around on two levels in a complete square, closed off on all sides. In the center was a completely empty expanse that went down to a floor level where he thought he saw movement. Basically, once he moved away from his position, there would be no cover, and all he could do was pray that no one looked up from the lower levels.

Again, he looked around the corner to the right of the elevator and was relieved to confirm that no one was on his level. However, the back wall on that right walkway was occupied by a ridiculous looking mass of cords, wires, and whatever else, some wider than Nigel, jumbled together and reaching straight up past any discernible distance. He considered walking over to them and concealing himself amongst them but was afraid of being seen along the way, because at this point, he could definitely hear voices. They were faint, impossible to distinguish. They came from below.

Crouching now, Nigel lay himself flat on the freezing metal floor and crawled forward until just his eyes were over the edge of the walkway. Below, on the cavern's bottom, below the second level of railings, was the strangest looking machine he had ever seen. While it stood prominently in the middle of the immense space, the primary apparatus only stood about seven and a half feet tall. It was shaped like a metal donut, and there was a purplish glow coming from its center. Surrounding the donut, thick, bent metal rods radiated around it, mimicking its shape and forming a kind of frame. Atop them was a metal cube, and below it was a long metal cylinder, supporting the main apparatus. While these were the basic components, the machine was wreathed in colorful copper tubes and yellow wires, blue cords and steel pipes, many of which continued out in every direction, reaching other complicated looking doohickeys. Five men and women walked from one piece of machinery to another, checking this and that. They were looking at dials and readouts, taking measurements, and periodically, they would ask each other questions or yell across the room. On the floor above them, below Nigel, a couple more people were moving around in sealed glass rooms that may have existed in any standard office. Nigel took pictures with his phone, pulling his face back from the edge as he did so. He zoomed in on the machine and snapped some pictures, then was preparing to take a video, when the flash went off on his camera. It lit up the entire cavern, and Nigel's gut churned in the way it only could when he did something monumentally stupid.

The entire company looked up at once to see where the flash had come from. By that time, Nigel was already sprinting into the elevator and jamming his finger on the button. More than anything, he wanted to take off his thick coat which was now making him uncomfortably hot. His pulse quickened as he heard yelling and some sort of clang that sounded like someone dropping a tuba. After fourteen presses, the elevator doors finally began to close, and Nigel breathed slowly out, his lips pursed, as it began to ascend.

He scrolled through his photos, trying to send them to headquarters, but he was too far underground for the signal to reach a satellite. After the longest amount of time Nigel had ever waited for anything, the doors opened once more. He expected security or someone to be waiting there to murder him, but the vault was empty. He sprang up the steps and closed the hatch, accidently slamming it with a *THUD*. He ran over and tried the door, but it did not open. *Typical!* He took off his shoe, made his grappling hook, and, with significantly more effort than the first time, he found his way to the top. He wriggled inside, placed the panel loosely back, then crawled through, even more conscious of the noise he was making than before.

He did not pause once, but instead crawled furiously at a continuous pace until he reached his original starting point. He popped the panel out. He looked around the red tinted storage room. Still there was no one. But that did nothing to slow the pace at which Nigel's heart was beating. From the beginning he had known this would be the hardest part, and he took comfort in the fact that, in his present circumstance, there was no one to blame but himself.

Nigel had trouble looping his cord around the ventilation pipe this time, since he had to do it around the one on which he was sitting. He was trying to muster enough torque to let momentum fling the shoe over and around, when he thought he heard footsteps from down the hall. Panicking, Nigel swiveled his head in every direction, finally making a decision no sane person would make, even in such a situation. He slid his way over to the wall where the pipe turned sharply down into the floor. Then, as the footsteps grew louder, he hugged it with all his body and slid down, holding on for dear life. There was a moment when his arm lost its purchase while he was accelerating, and he almost fell. But a half a second later he was collapsed onto solid ground. He survived, albeit, with a sprained ankle.

After crashing into the floor like a bag of garbage, he took two steps, pried open the door with the strength of two men, and fell into the snow, the door closing behind him, not having been opened even halfway. He checked the time. There was still at least forty minutes left until the building reopened. After the noise of the underground cavern, the still, Antarctic darkness was uncomfortably quiet. Nigel moved as quickly as he could toward the snowmobiles, his muscles aching and his ankle ablaze with pain. In hindsight, he realized that he should have just left one of the snowmobiles with the security team. He was just having one of those days.

Surprised to find no opposition, he commandeered the largest snowmobile he could find, which was more of a small truck than anything. He called ahead, and by the time he made it to the plane, the UN team was outside waiting for him. One of them quietly shook his head as Nigel pulled up. "Got something to say?" Nigel asked him.

"No," said the security officer quietly.

"Yeah dude, better keep it to yourself." Nigel gestured toward the rest of them and the snowmobile. "Pile in. I gotta do something real fast."

Nigel went inside the plane and took a pee that lasted longer than might be expected. He then uploaded the pictures he had taken, backing them up to his section of the UN database. Finally, he called the United Nations' technical research department directly, giving his name, badge number, and case filing number, the latter, Tom had thankfully forwarded him. It was a temporary filing number, since it had been pushed through so quickly, and Nigel made a note to keep track of it.

A disheveled looking man, who from lack of sleep probably looked older than he was, appeared onscreen, making Nigel wish the screen were not so big. "Hello, this is Jeffery in research," said the man.

"Yeah, it's Nigel."

The man squinted at Nigel, but clearly did not know who he was. "Yeah? Do you need to talk to somebody?"

"Jeezus, I just went through all this. Don't you have any of the information I just submitted?"

The man rolled his eyes and moved off-screen, typing something. He came back in view, his face a less haggard version of its previous self. "Oh hey! You're the box guy!" The man's eyes had lit up to seven-year-old at theme-park levels.

"Um, yeah, I guess. Did you find anything?"

"Well, that's a complicated answer. Don't you work homicide though? Where did you find this?"

"Hey! I'm the one with the questions. We're a little short on time here."

"Fine. Well, once we realized what we were looking at with some of these diagrams, we had to call in some experts on nuclear reactions and engineering."

"And?"

"And, well, everything is written in some kind of code or something, and the digital files are all encrypted. Now, there's still no luck with the paper stuff, but the IT guys cut right through those ancient encryptions, no problem. Anyway, based on the engineering specs, we think we might have a holy grail on our hands."

At this point, Nigel could see other members of the department crowded around Jefferey, watching pensively from a distance. "What exactly does that mean?"

Jeffery paused, not sure how to respond. He looked up at some of his coworkers that stood outside the camera's range and nodded at them. He turned back toward Nigel. "We think it might be the big one, now we're not sure yet, so—"

"Come on, spit it out."

"We think it's detailed plans for a nuclear fusion reactor. We think that, at the very least, if we can crack this code, it'll advance our research. We've been so close for decades."

Nigel stroked his chin. "Fusion... that's the world saving, global warming fixing one, right?"

Jefferey gave a condescending, enthusiastic, excited, exasperated, and resounding "Yes!"

"Okay then, Jeff, since I got you on the horn, maybe this will help. I took some pictures connected to the case I'm working, maybe they'll help. Do I give them to you?"

"Dear lord, yes please. That's absolutely fine, I can sign them in for you."

Nigel sent the pictures across. Immediately, Jefferey's eyes grew wide and his mouth fell open. He tried to speak, but no sound came out.

"Well? Yes, no?"

"We'll um, yeah we can take a look." The screen went blank.

"What the hell is it with people hanging up on me?" Nigel fumed.

Nigel went back outside to find a cold and miserable company of peacekeepers on the verge of mutiny. "What?" he asked. "I'm over here saving the world and slamming down the hammer of justice. I think you can handle a little bit of cold, especially considering the alternative. Now let's go catch us a bad guy."

CHAPTER XVII

THE YEAR 2076

Nigel drove the snow truck, calling Oslow and Catherine on the way, telling them to meet him at the entrance to the main building. Taking a detour, Nigel woke Carl and brought him along. Then he knocked on Alexi's door. Alexi answered, fully dressed and already awake. After a bit of convincing, Alexi piled into the truck as well. They were at capacity, if not past it, and as Nigel settled back into the driver's seat, an image of a clown car sprang to mind. During the short trip, Carl complained loudly and often about the cramped conditions, asking what was going on. Alexi remained silent.

Outside the building's entrance, Oslow and

Catherine were once again waiting for Nigel's return. Before Nigel had completely slowed the truck to a stop, three of his peacekeepers had already jumped out, awkwardly flinging themselves into the snow. The rest piled out as soon as he had parked.

Catherine spoke first. "Detective, what is happening, who are these people?"

Nigel stood proudly in front of the group he had brought. "These are UN officers. They're here to transport our murder suspect. I wanted everyone here so we could all be on the same page."

Catherine looked carefully at Carl and Alexi. "And who is suspect you have?"

"Could we do this inside?" Nigel asked, his nose red. The building was, for the time being, still locked down. "You can get us in as the supervisor, right?"

"Okay," she said. "We can go inside."

She called her security team to let them know she was going in, then opened the front entrance. As they filed inside, Carl came up to Nigel. "What the bloody hell happened to you mate? You look like the bottom of an empty dumpster."

Confused, Nigel noticed the thick layer of dirt

and grime that covered the front of his outfit. "Uh, long story." He brushed Carl off. "Go be British somewhere else dude, you're hurting my ears."

Once everyone had entered, Oslow grabbed a chair and began to sit. "No need," said Nigel. "This shouldn't take long." Oslow shrugged and pushed the chair back in. Nigel spoke again, addressing the room which Catherine had turned on the proper lights to, instead of leaving their conversation drenched in an ominous red. "As you know, I found a knife at the crime scene. Based on its depth in the snow and the fact that it was probably dropped, it was left around the time of the murder. There wasn't blood or anything on it, and Anton wasn't stabbed, but—"

"Exactly," Catherine broke in. "That can be no use for you. It has nothing to do with death of Anton."

"Yo! Will you let me finish? I'm getting there."

Catherine nodded apologetically.

"Anyway," Nigel continued, "there were some nylon rope fibers stuck in a chip on the blade, and some clear prints." Nigel turned to look behind him. Alexi and Carl were standing side by side, and the UN security team was behind them, blocking the door. Nigel walked up to Alexi, whose nostrils were flared, and stood directly in front of him as he kept speaking. "They belonged to a Russian government agent who has been a wanted international criminal for the last sixty years." Nigel drew a fingerprint scanner from his coat and held it out. He tried to grab the old man's hand. "Alexi, if you'll let me—" Alexi yanked his hand violently back, the peacekeepers stepping forward as he did so. Nigel waved them off. "That's fine, we don't need to do that now." Alexi glanced behind him, aware of the officers' presence.

Nigel turned back toward Oslow and Catherine. Oslow's face was plastered with utter astonishment. Nigel continued, "I did some digging on this guy whose prints were on the knife. He was charged with manslaughter. The manslaughter of a woman who was working on something for a company essentially run by the Russian government. For whatever reason, she decided to stop working for them. The man, whose real name is Rurik, was instructed to cover up whatever she had been working on, or to maybe even retrieve something she'd stolen."

Carl asked, "What does this have to do with—"

"Guys are you serious?" shouted Nigel. "You're ruining my flow. Save questions for the end."

When Carl was done rolling his eyes, Nigel thought for a moment, eventually picking up his story once more. "I submit to you"—Nigel pointed his finger in the air as dramatically as possible—"that the same thing has happened once more. Fleeing the law of the land and absconding from the US with the help of the Russian government, Rurik continued his nefarious work for many years. Finally, being one of the few agents with knowledge of the highly protected secret project Russia was guarding for decades, Rurik was assigned here, to this research station, where the project was being brought to fruition and tested in secret. And I further submit"—Nigel lowered his finger until it was pointed at Alexi's chest—"that this man is in fact, Rurik Kuznetsov!"

Rurik' pruney face was crimson at the cheeks. "How dare you! I am leaving. You have no proof of this. You are a child, so don't waste my time with childishness and nonsense." He addressed Catherine. "I expect to be treated with more respect."

Nigel smiled. "Well, if you're innocent, we can find that out easy enough. But until then, thanks to my buddies back there, nobody's going anywhere. Here's what I think pal. I think that you were keeping an eye on things. I think everything was going just fine until this new wave of immigrants showed up. You just had to report back that everything was going smoothly. But it wasn't, was it? You noticed Anton sneaking in through the back after closing. He probably found something one day doing his job working maintenance, and he was getting closer to learning your precious secret. First, you got closer to Anton, squared everything so you were reassigned as his roommate. When you realized he was sneaking off every night, you probably found photos he had taken of that room with the cameras. So, you had to make a quick decision before he spilled the beans. You stole his knife so you could have two. One to stab him, and one to show someone like me who came looking. You'd stab poor Anton in the dark when he snuck in after closing. You'd be waiting for him in the storage room. Then you'd steal every device of his that had the photos, and report back to your people that the problem was fixed."

The shriveled old man was staring Nigel dead in the eyes, unmoving, his fists clenched. Oslow looked like he was having a hard time buying the story. Oslow asked, "But how would he have been able to be assigned to Anton's unit? He didn't request it, we asked him to move."

"Aha," said Nigel. "Which brings me to my next point."

"Oh, I get it, so he's allowed to ask questions but I'm not?" Carl snapped

"Jeezus, shut up Carl. Where was I, um, oh yeah, so, as we all know, Anton's neck was broken, he wasn't stabbed. There was someone else who knew about Anton's nightly adventures, someone Rurik was reporting to." Nigel began walking across the wide room, straight through to the corridor. "If you would all come with me, there is something I think you all should see."

The group moved into the storage room where the body was found, and where Nigel had been crawling around such a short time before. They formed a circle with Nigel at the center and UN officers at the corridor entrance and the back door. Nigel picked up where he had left off. "Anton was coming in through this backdoor which, as you can see," Nigel said, pushing the guards out of the way to demonstrate the ritual of its opening, "Is either intentionally or unintentionally broken. My money's on intentionally, Anton needed a way in, and he would have known how to get it to open."

"Why?" asked Oslow.

"It was like you said, Carl," Nigel responded. "Anton found something kooky going on while he was doing his maintenance work. This tube here, if someone could get inside and follow it all the way down, it would bring that foolish person inside the locked room down the hall with the guards and cameras. Have any of you been in that room?" asked Nigel, directing his question at Catherine, Oslow, and Carl. "Well our buddy Anton made it in there, or at least had a look inside. Carl, let me ask, did you ever see Anton in one of these?" Nigel asked, picking up one of the blue harnesses from a box.

"Yeah, all the time. That's how he did a lot of the work that was too high up for a ladder."

"And that's also how he was getting into the vents. These harnesses and cords are made from nylon rope, and I'll bet they'll be a match for the fibers on that knife." Nigel's audience still looked a little confused but were starting to catch on. "Rurik's plan was to hide in here, then cut Anton down once he was twenty feet up in the air. While he was in shocked from the fall, probably with broken legs, Rurik would already be on top of him, stabbing him, and no one would be the wiser. But that's not what happened either is it? Is it Rurik? Rurik?" Nigel spun in a tight circle, the peacekeepers looking around dumbly as well. "Where did he go? Where is he? You have one job to do! For Putin's sake, the man is over a hundred years old!" Everyone looked back into the room they'd just left, which was completely empty. "You two idiots, go find him or none of us are going to afford groceries next month." The two Peacekeepers by the door sprinted off.

Nigel turned back to the group, continuing his story in an exasperated tone. "Anyway. Wait, where was I? The knife, the vent..."

"The harness," Oslow added helpfully.

Nigel was back on track. "Okay yeah. Rurik couldn't have gotten in here alone; he didn't have a passkey. Even if he did—"

"It wouldn't have worked," Carl finished. "Which reminds me," Carl held out his hand. Nigel rooted around in his pocket, pulling out the cube Carl had given him. Catherine looked on in horror as he plopped it back into Carl's hand.

Once again, Nigel picked up where he left off. "I doubt he could have opened that heavy door by himself, let alone, held it open while dragging Anton's three-hundred-pound body out into the snow. The only person who could have let him in was you, Catherine."

All eyes were now on Catherine. The two guards who had stayed looked like all they needed was some popcorn. "What are you saying?" Catherine began to object.

"I'm saying that you're the supervisor. You're in charge of this entire facility, you've been here as long as anyone. You know what's going on behind that door, and you were told to keep it under wraps, or they'd throw you, and anyone else they had to, in a hole where no one would find you. Maybe they told you it was a matter of national security, something like that. Am I getting warmer?"

Catherine was sweating profusely, and Nigel knew he had won. She said, "I don't know, what are you talking—"

Nigel stalked forward, not breaking eye contact. "*You* knew about those extra employees, *you* re-zoned Rurik, *you* knew about those cameras, *you* lied about the knife and, might I add, even tried to throw sweet, innocent Carl under the bus for it." Catherine backed slowly against the wall, peacekeepers now on either side of her. "Thanks to Rurik, you knew what Anton was up to, and you two figured you could handle it yourselves by murdering him. You both snuck in here, cut the counterweight on his rope, but when he fell, he broke his neck. In the heat of the moment, you decided to stick with the original plan to throw him out into the snow, drawing attention away from what he was doing there in the middle of the night, and the building itself. And I'm sure somewhere there's a record in the computer of who opened up the building with her passkey in the middle of the night." Catherine bowed her head as the UN officers put her in handcuffs. "But there's one thing you didn't count on, Cat." Catherine remained silent, not taking the bait. "And that was having such a handsome and clever detective on the case."

Out of absolutely nowhere, a smack echoed off the walls as Carl openhand slapped Catherine full across the face, twisting his body for maximum effect. "Woah!" Nigel yelled, as a peacekeeper stepped forward. But by then, Oslow was wrestling Carl back. Nigel would have laughed, had Carl not started sobbing into Oslow's shoulder.

Outside, Nigel radioed in for a report from the two officers who had gone chasing after Rurik. Apparently, they had seen him speed off toward the plane in a snowmobile and were just now catching up. *I'm gonna have to talk to Tom about our hiring policies*. Nigel thought.

"Hey genius!" Nigel yelled at a handcuffed Rurik once everyone had made it back to the jet. "The plane is autopilot. It won't fly without my say so."

Rurik spat in the snow at Nigel's feet.

CHAPTER XVIII

THE YEAR 2076

Back at United Nations headquarters, Nigel left his suspects behind for detainment and went to the locker room for a shower and a change of clothes. After his shower, while Nigel was trying to find his pants, Tom walked in. Seeing Tom, Nigel groaned loudly. "Please not now. I need a nap."

Tom, dressed in an expensive Italian suit, said, "I don't know what you did, but I just met with the director. Tom held out his hand. "I'm going to need those photos you took."

Nigel, while doubled over, searching distractedly under a bench for his pants said, "Sure, whatever. I'll send those to you after my nap."

"The originals, Nigel. We need IT to confirm

them authentic before we start an international incident."

Nigel stood up, still pants-less. "Um, what?"

"The research team came to me with what you gave them. I passed it up the ladder. The director wants you onboard a plane to Russia by end of day."

"Woah, woah, back up. Why? And more importantly, am I getting paid overtime?"

"Let me put it this way, you're either getting a promotion or being fired. Apparently, they said those pictures you took matched the earliest files from that box you handed me. They are plans for a nuclear fusion reactor small enough to fit in a truck and power an entire city. No waste, no radiation byproducts."

"Wait, so, did they crack the code?"

"No. But it looks liked the later files might be for an upgraded version, smaller and more efficient."

"Those plans must've been what the bad guys were after."

"Regardless, if the Russian government has been building and actively burying, functioning fusion reactors, you'd better believe we have something to say. They're not getting away with this shit."

"What about my case? D'you really think Russia is gonna put them in the slammer if we tip them off that we know about all this? They're still Russian citizens, right?"

Tom screwed up his mouth and put his hands in his pockets. "I figure it's about fifty/fifty. If our courts find them guilty, Russia will want them back to make sure they don't talk. Based on the circumstances, we should be able to block it for a while. But with the old guy, if we don't try him at all, he's still wanted in the US. So, he won't go down for your murder, but we can negotiate it with the US to keep him locked up here indefinitely."

"Keep an eye on him. Make sure you know who he's talking to," Nigel warned.

"Why?"

"Because he's a Russian spy, duh. Haven't you been reading my reports?"

"You haven't submitted any!"

"Oh. Yeah." Nigel resumed the search for his pants.

Tom grumbled something and started walking

out. "Hand over those pictures once you get some clothes on. And you can nap on the plane."

After a longer amount of time than it should have taken, Nigel found his pants. At the sight of them, Nigel was not as happy as he should have been, for he knew it portended a long and messy trip which he was unequipped to fully understand the ramifications of. Nigel handed his camera off to the person Tom had left waiting outside the locker room to collect it. Then, he went down to the research department, asking Jefferey for his personal contact number in case Nigel had any questions. He also told Jeffery to let him know immediately if they found anything else useful from the box.

In no time at all, Nigel found himself on a new, even fancier plane. With him was the director of the United Nations (whose full name was forgotten by Nigel every time he asked for it), Tom, and a diplomatic envoy who was also the United Nation's top Russian representative. The envoy had not been briefed. Nigel, trying to catch a few winks in the rearmost seat of the cabin, glanced up at the director every once and a while when the angry whispers she exchanged with Tom grew to speaking volume before quickly falling back down. She was incredibly young to be in the position she was, at the head of the most powerful governing body in the world. Although no one ever said it, she was the most powerful person in the world, and though her hazelnut hair caught the light just so, Nigel kept his distance. Behind her, the pasty and underfed Russian representative sat, doing his best impression of a person who was not eavesdropping.

The plane landed, and not knowing the time it had taken to arrive, Nigel was not entirely sure whether he had fallen asleep or not. If he had, it was a shallow and unsatisfying experience, much like his victory over the Antarctic murderers.

Coming off the plane, the group was invited into the Kremlin Senate, a building which Nigel found to be both imposing and beautifully constructed. Its columns supported a central cylindrical structure, atop which stood a proud flag. On two sides, flat walls with three stories of windows jutted out at a ninety-degree angle from the cylinder. Within the area which the entire structure bordered, a wide and empty courtyard extended, which took forever and a day to cross. As they were walking in, Nigel felt a cool breeze glide across his cheek. He expected the Russian winter to be colder than it was, but the climate could be described more as fair and balmy than anything else.

The four of them were guided through an exquisitely decorated interior, into a room with a wide mahogany desk and a massive crystal chandelier. They were instructed to sit and wait in front of the president's desk until he arrived and were offered drinks. Everyone refused except Nigel, who asked for a black coffee. Nigel was on the far right, sitting next to Tom. Tom leaned over and said, "I need you to do something for me." He looked serious.

"What's that?"

"Say nothing. Keep quiet, and don't talk to the president."

"Then why am I here?"

Just then, the Russian president walked in from the door behind them, wearing a blue suit and no tie. Everyone stood, and the president shook everyone's hands one at a time, starting with the director and ending with Nigel, who was clearly unknown to him. The president took his seat across from them. "I was just informed of the little incident at our research base. Thank you for clearing that up. Is that why you've come?"

"In part, yes," said the director, having done away with the air of pleasantries she had temporarily assumed. "Mr. President, during our investigation, one of our detectives found something quite disturbing. It looks like this nationally sanctioned research team of yours is working on what seems to be an active nuclear fusion reactor."

The president's eyebrows raised a little, but he betrayed no real emotion. He laced his fingers together in front of his chin, resting his elbows on the desk. "That's quite ridiculous. Maybe this investigator of yours mistook what he saw. If anything, they were probably simply doing fusion research."

Tom took out the camera which Nigel had given him and smacked it down on the desk. He pressed a button, and it projected a picture of the reactor in the air in front of the president's face. The president squinted at it and chuckled. "Well that could be anything. Like I said, I am sure our researchers are hard at work trying to find a cure for the planet's ails. Now—"

"Then why is it powering the entire research

base?" Nigel bluffed, recalling what Carl told him of Anton's suspicions.

The tension in the room notched itself up to a ten. The president looked at the strange little man who was probably the first person in decades to sit in that office without wearing a sport coat. He was also the only one in the group not sitting in a rigidly uncomfortable position, instead, slouching in his chair. The president sneered. "And who are you again?"

Tom kicked Nigel under the table and said, "This is our lead investigator, Detective Nigel Woods. He brought this to our attention. He's also the one who solved the murder case."

"Well Detective Woods, you are misinformed. Our research stations use h—"

"Then why was a Russian spy given permission to assassinate him? Rurik Kuznetsov?"

Tom winced. Nigel continued, "We know that's a nuclear reactor. Your spy gave away the plans that Truskol was trying to steal back before the company shut down."

The president tapped his finger rhythmically on the desk. "This is complete nonsense. Whatever you think you have found is nothing but gossip and lies. As you can see"—he stretched out his arms—"we have built no new nuclear plants. Inspect any of the ones we have, and you will find fission processes only. No fusion. Were we to truly use this new form of nuclear energy, which the scientific community has been unsuccessfully trying to develop for a century, we would share it with the global community. My country is just as much affected by the global climate catastrophe as any other and the world has suffered enough. We, like everyone, want to put a stop to it right away."

The director spoke up in an even tone, lowering the overall volume in the room. "But that's not strictly true, is it?" she said.

"What isn't?" said the president, tapping at a persistently increasing rate.

"Your nation is not just as much affected as every other country. Russia is the coldest country on the planet. If anything, it has increased your internal revenue, especially concerning agricultural production. The world economy is collapsing, but your nation seems to be doing just fine. In fact, this is now the most powerful nation in the world, by any metric. A big part of that is the fact that you spend far less on energy and fuels than any of the larger nations, claiming that you've been using more renewable forms of energy.

"Let's say you had nuclear fusion energy. Sixty percent of your exports are mineral fuels including oil. Just over the last few years, the biggest glacial passes have melted, giving you unprecedented trade access to North America. If you sat on this discovery, you would only gain in power until you were ready to sell the technology to the highest bidder, becoming the most powerful nation in human history. If by then it's not too late, of course. Hypothetically, a sociopathic, perverted mind would consider it an economically smarter move to bury the technology, only using it in secret. I'd say that's a secret worth killing over, wouldn't you?"

Startled, Nigel realized the last question was directed at him, as she turned to face him, her blue eyes sparkling with the brilliance of a thousand stars. Nigel's pulse quickened to an alarming level, and in that moment, he fell in love. *Emma,* came the name, shoving itself into the front of his mind.

"Sir," said a voice from behind, as he was tapped on the shoulder. It was the waiter or butler or someone, bringing Nigel his coffee. He took it, mumbling "Thank you," or a phrase of the like.

When Nigel looked up, Director Emma's attention was now reaffixed to the president who was still as coolheaded as ever. "Even if these hateful lies were true," he said, "that technology would be the property of Russia, to do with as we please."

Emma did not seem to take that well. She stood up, pointing at the holographic picture still hanging in the air. "Dammit! Do you have any idea what we deal with every day? The amount of people who die in floods, in hurricanes, burnt in fires? This isn't about your nation's laws. This is a moral failing! Crime has no time zones anymore. This is a problem that affects all of us, and it's an evil, despicable crime against humanity itself."

Over the course of her speech, a vein had arisen on Emma's forehead, and it pulsed with the blood of a warrior. Nigel thought it was the most beautiful thing he had ever seen, and were he a painter, he would spend the rest of his life trying to immortalize it in the techniques of his ancestors.

The president stood as well, matching Emma's stance. Leaning on the desk, he pointed toward the door. "If there is nothing else, it's time for you to leave."

Emma smacked the desk, and Tom retrieved

the camera, turning it off. The envoy sat meekly in his chair, unsure of what to do. The president nodded at him, and the envoy also stood to leave. The only one not standing was Nigel, who did not want his coffee going to waste. He tried to gulp it down quickly but stopped after receiving a vicious burn on his tongue.

They walked briskly from the building, Nigel who, having left his coffee, took up the rear. They walked in silence. On the plane, Nigel rushed rudely past Tom, taking his seat next to Emma. She took a call as the plane ascended, and Nigel waited patiently for her to finish. A few minutes later, she ended the conversation and he said, "You know, I think what you were saying was—"

"WHAT the HELL was THAT?!" Tom shouted, standing between Nigel and the director, steadying himself on their seats.

"What?"

Tom's eyes widened. "I told you not to say anything!"

"Oh, get off it Tom," said Emma. "Go sit down."

Tom glared but went back to his seat.

"That was brave of you," said Emma, a much kinder person than Nigel had imagined.

"Thanks, I— ow."

"What's wrong?"

"Oh nothing, I just burnt my tongue. I couldn't believe how hot that coffee was. It was like they made it dangerously hot on purpose. They must've pulled it out of the pot and heated it up again or something." Emma was prepared to speak, but the expression that suddenly grew on Nigel's face gave her pause. His eyes grew wide and vacant, and his mouth, burnt tongue and all, fell open. "Wait... hold up a second. Um," he pointed to the back of the plane. "I have a couple phone calls to make. Give me a sec."

He made his way to the back, dialing Jefferey's private line first. "Yo Jeff."

"Who's this?"

"Detective Nigel. Question: you told Tom that the more recent plans from that box were for a smaller fusion reactor, right?"

"It looks like it. Without a codex, it's hard to know the measurements for sure. But it seems like an all-around significant improvement."

"How small are we talking?"

"Um, let me get a consensus." Nigel was put on hold and heard murmurs in the background of the audio call. He paced in a small circle, turning back toward the front to see Tom and Emma leaning over their seats staring back at him. The envoy was snoring loudly. Jeffery's voice reemerged. "So, they're saying it could be, if the design were actually feasible, as small as a meter, maybe not quite as powerful as the bigger version. No less amazing, obviously."

Nigel hung up and immediately put in a call to Liza, grateful he still had her information.

"Hello?" she said.

"Hi, it's Detective Nigel. I have just one quick question for you,"

"Oh, hi detective. How can I help you?"

"Yeah so, the house in Florida. Are you paying the electric bill on that by any chance?"

"Um, no, I think they told me a while ago that they were shutting off the power. Why do you—" Nigel hung up and stumbled to the front of the cabin. Tom and Emma both waited for whatever news he was clearly about to share.

"We need to land in Florida."

"And why in God's name would we do that?" asked Tom, clearly averse to the idea.

"I think I know where to find a reactor."

Emma looked confused. "In Florida?"

"Come on guys, we need to change course."

Tom was once more about to object, but Emma walked to the cockpit to reinstruct the autopilot. The fasten seatbelt sign came on.

————————————

At the abandoned Florida airstrip, Nigel assured them they would not have to get off and instructed them to keep the air conditioning on. No one bothered to wake the envoy.

Nigel took, what was probably, the same automatic car as before, to Liza's old home. Walking with the expedience of a man who needs to do something important but would rather not have a heatstroke, he burst through the front door, and was greeted once more by the sweet embrace of cold air in a house on a block with no power. He closed the door and stood where he had entered, taking a long, slow look around. Logically, whatever was powering the house would probably have wires coming out of it. His spirits fell as he realized it could be hidden in the walls. But that too would only delay him.

He walked into the kitchen and turned on the light. Because there was no time on the old microwave oven, and because the house was owned by reasonable people, Nigel had assumed the appliances were unplugged. But the light came on when he opened the ancient refrigerator door, and it was still as cold as the day it was purchased. A significant amount of frost had built up in the freezer section, but otherwise, it was empty. Thrusting his entire body, he moved it away from the wall and looked behind. He saw nothing he would consider out of the ordinary and moved on.

He moved an empty cardboard box off the stovetop and saw with horror that the stove's digital clock was displaying the time. He cursed his own stupidity for not having checked it when he entered the house originally. He slid over to the microwave, which was either broken or... Nigel pushed the eject button. It did not open. He carefully pulled it away from the wall, and to his great joy, saw a row of exceptionally thick cords leading back behind the countertop. He made the call.

CHAPTER XIX

EPILOGUE

Nigel arrived at the house late. He was still a little hungover from the night before, and it took him a while to leave his front door. But he had arrived, late as he was, although day was soon to become night. He walked up to the front door of the quaint two-story home with bright blue vinyl siding. The door was ajar. "Come in!" sang a voice from within.

Nigel walked across the pale-yellow carpet and sat on the blue couch. To his left sat a worn leather armchair, faded and cracked, that Nigel somehow had not noticed on his first visit. Upon it, sat the ninety-two-year-old Liza. "Have some lemonade," she said, gesturing toward a pitcher on the low coffee table in front of him.

"Sure," said Nigel, obligingly pouring himself a generous glass.

"You remind me of my husband," she said, nursing her own glass.

Nigel laughed. "Oh really, how's that?"

"I don't know, the way you carry yourself. Maybe it's a detective thing."

"Maybe."

"So."

"So," Nigel said, putting down his glass. "Your grandmother, Hazel, she was a helluva lady."

"Last time we spoke, you said that her microwave was a nuclear fusion reactor and she had stolen her work back from the Russian government. I think that might be an understatement."

"Well, government adjacent, but yes. What was that, about a month ago now?"

"I think so."

"I came here in person because I wanted to be the first to give you the news. With her microwave, the geeks were able to reverse engineer her notes. The UN now has specs for fusion reactors that far outpace the early model she built for Truskol. The ones Russia was using. We've started production and we're starting to distribute to the biggest countries with the most infrastructure."

"Oh my god."

"I thought you should know. Without you and without her, I mean she was a hero."

"Why'd she have to run from them though?"

Nigel gazed out the window at the golden rays of a setting sun. "I think she knew they were going to bury her work. Based on what Nate wrote, she was an activist way before she started working for them."

Liza grinned and nodded. "That sounds like her. I think what you've accomplished is the reason she took the job in the first place." Liza laughed. "It just took a little longer than she expected."

"They put her picture up in the memorial hall if you ever stop by. There've been talks of a posthumous humanitarian award, maybe a Nobel." He shrugged. "If these things work as efficiently as that microwave does." Nigel stood up. "Well, I should get going."

Liza came over to say goodbye, and Nigel held out his hand. She ignored it, giving him a colossal hug, almost bowling him over. "You did this," she said, squeezing him with all the strength she could muster. "Thank you. Thank you for trying." She pulled away, holding him at arm's length. "This is as much her as it was you. You should be proud of yourself."

"I always am," said Nigel, opening the door.

THE END

SPECIAL THANKS TO:
Tyrell
Nana
Josh
Tyler
Geoff
Monique
And, you know, other people probably.

Lightning Source UK Ltd.
Milton Keynes UK
UKHW040044240421
382498UK00010B/279